PRINTHOUSE BOOKS PRESENTS

I0672700

A Mere Reality

FICTION

Rollie C. Gray, Jr.

Urban Literature

© 2016 Rollie C. Gray, Jr.

Editor: Cheryl Hinton

PrintHouse Books, Atlanta, GA.

Published 5-15-2016

www.PrintHouseBooks.com

VIP INK Publishing Group; Incorporated

This novel is fiction but also has been inspired by true events, most characters are fictitious no matter how true the event. Some characters remained the same as the events have been documented to the public and are on public record.

"A Mere Reality"

Cover art designed by Beyond Graphix

ISBN: 978-0-9970016-79

Library of Congress Cataloging-in-Publication Data

#2016935708

A Mere Reality

1. Drama 2.Hip Hop 3. Romance 4.Urban Literature 5. Rollie C. Gray, Jr.

Printed in the United States of America

Rollie C. Gray, Jr.

A Mere Reality

VIP INK Publishing Group, Incorporated

Atlanta, GA.

Strickland, a B-Boy from the Southside of Chicago grew up in the 80's and 90's during the golden era of Hip-Hop; rhyming and battling on the Chi-Town streets prepared him to take over what would become a billion dollar industry. During the late 90's America changed and Hip-Hop followed suit. There was an influx of money in Hip-Hop, but it came with a cost.

Hip-Hop became darker, and Strickland became darker with it. He had to make a decision to contribute to society or add to its demise. What happens when you speak the truth? What happens when you mention the elephant in the room? You suddenly realize that what you believed to be true is nothing more than a mere reality.

Rollie C. Gray

**A Chicago Hip-Hop Story...**

"A Mere Reality"

www.PrinthouseBooks.com

"A Mere Reality"

In loving memory of Laura Gray and Rollie Gray Sr.

Table of Contents

Part I: Going Down

Chapter 1

You never thought that hip-hop would take it this far...

I AM AN AMERICAN, CHICAGO BORN —
CHICAGO, THAT UNCOMPROMISING
CITY. Harveyl Strickland is my name and this
is my story; a story about the trials and
tribulations of a B-Boy that found the love of
himself, his people, and a woman by way of an
art form known as hip-hop.

I had made it. The director's Louis
Vuitton loafers and the plaques on the wall of
multi-platinum artists was a clear indicator.
As Sprite's marketing executive began to make
his speech in the trendy office on 28th & Park
Ave, the chatters of success came to a halt. The
top shelf liquor and the reeking smell of
marijuana creeping in from the patio below at
High Times Magazine distracted me.

Afterwards Tyler and I walked to Radio City Music Hall for a final walk through; it was a cool summer night so I opted out of driving, walking gave me an opportunity to relish the moment. Following the walk through we proceeded downstairs to the gathering for the artists performing in the concert.

Boost mobile and Sprite went all out for this one and the promotions were crazy. They had partnership with MTV and Clear Channel; the concerts were scheduled for New York, Atlanta, and California. For a new artist this was major, Tyler really pulled it off. Later that night I sat in my apartment overlooking Time Square and reflected on how I got there from the south side of Chicago.

As I sat on the edge of my bed smoking an American Spirit, I reminisced about my first place of residency which was Englewood, a neighborhood in Chicago located on the south side. I laughed to myself thinking that if the childhood homies knew that I smoked cigarettes with an Indian as a logo, and claimed to be organic and natural, I am sure they would ridicule me and tell me to go buy a pack of Newport shorts.

I lived on 65th & Peoria between the 63rd & Halsted train station and Ogden Park. I stayed in a poorly structured wooden building on the second floor with my parents, all four of my sisters, an occasional brother, uncle, aunt, or friend. My family was a typical family in the Englewood area. I had an alcoholic uncle that you constantly saw in the neighborhood, a brother that was a Gangster Disciple, a rescue dog, strong mother, and a father doing his best to hold it together.

Everyone in the hood knew each other and, for the most part, looked out for the *block*. Still to this day I am never Strickland- to the block I'm always "such and such little brother." Another part of my extended family was the church. The story goes as such. There was a vacant lot on 65th and Carpenter, a few blocks from the crib. My sister Elizabeth used to play there until a church was built on the property. The name of the church was Original Philadelphia Missionary Baptist Church. Elizabeth became a member and the family followed suit. We would go to church all the time, all day Sunday, Sunday school, morning service, Baptist Training Union, Bible Study, funerals, etc.

Two experiences stand out about church. I remember asking my Sunday school teacher why the pictures of Jesus were white. Her response was that Jesus had no color. That answer never set well with me. The second incident was when I realized that all men weren't interested in women. The church had an all night revival and in the morning we all went outside to get some air. I heard a man say that he could not wait to see his man. Needless to say, that confused me, and after that I viewed him and the church differently and from that moment on I kept my distance from both.

I always enjoyed the music at church, the live instruments, acoustic piano, bass guitar, organ, drums, tambourine, and the choir. Each Sunday morning the choir would line up on each side of the church wearing maroon and gold robes. The music would begin to play and the choir would begin to sing while marching down the aisle.

On Sundays if I wasn't singing in the youth choir I would sit in the balcony next to the drummer. I would sit to his right and an older lady named Donna would sit to his left. Each Sunday she would catch the *Holy Ghost*. The best way I can describe the Holy Ghost is a euphoric feeling that comes over you. It affects people in different ways, some folks cry, some go into a deep prayer. Usually this would happen after a good song or sermon.

I guess the Holy Ghost is contagious because people would catch it at the same time. This was the best time in church for me.

The drummer would begin to play faster, a woman would run down the middle aisle, another woman would begin dancing between the rows, several people in the choir would begin to scream, cry, and only the gifted ones would begin *speaking in tongues*. Some say that speaking in tongue is a divine language, the language of heaven or the language of the angels.

Now Donna would jump up and it appeared as if she was having an epileptic seizure. She was a very heavyset woman; she would jump up and down swinging her arms wildly near the edge of the balcony. Two men would attempt to restrain her to prevent her from falling off the balcony. The haters would whisper that she was faking and that you can't hurt yourself while in the spirit. In retrospect this was my first introduction to entertainment. Whether those folks were faking or not it was pure entertainment.

During the week I would go to choir rehearsal with my sisters, something I really enjoyed. Everyone was much more relaxed and informal, laughing, joking…just happy to be there. I would get so excited when the director of the choir would say that he wrote a new song and see it all come together, this is where I learned how to compose a song. It also was my introduction to hip-hop. After being at church all day Sunday Elizabeth would get home and play "Flash Light" by the Parliament, Sly and the Family Stone, the Isley Brothers, Heat Wave, and Kurtis Blow's "The Breaks".

I was being exposed to different types of music. My oldest sister Ethel would rock me to sleep on her lap while listening to slow jams; I can still hear the scratches and popping on the overplayed records. Music was always my closest and dearest friend. In church I learned the power of expression and that the human spirit loves to be entertained. So I took that and ran with it. This was around the time I began writing rap songs.

Chapter 2

What happens to a dream deferred?

IN 1968 THE ENGLEWOOD AREA OF
CHICAGO WAS DEVASTATED BY THE
MARTIN LUTHER KING RIOT WHICH
ENDED THE CIVIL RIGHTS ERA. In the 70's
came the black power movement, followed by
the hip-hop movement of the 80's. Hip-hop in
its early stage was a tool for urban youths to
express social and economical ills that were
prevalent in their communities.

Fortunately my family and I moved
further east on 81st & Cornell, which in my
eyes was a lot better than Englewood. I
transferred to Charles P. Caldwell elementary
school near 87th & Stony Island Ave. Caldwell
was like all schools on the south side, nothing
but remodeled industrial factory buildings.
New to the neighborhood I had to identify
with something and that something was hip-
hop.

Caldwell is where I was introduced to
Mrs. Lewis; she was my sixth and seventh
grade teacher. I was in room 107 with Adero,
Anthony, Mike, Darnel, Shannon, Yusef,
Lavita, Skye, Carla, Dionne, Kenya, etc. The

older white teachers who had been around since the days Caldwell was full of Polish kids, couldn't handle us. There was something about Mrs. Lewis, it was like you couldn't pull no B.S. on her, you could try but she would always call you on it, and nobody likes to be called on their bullshit.

Mrs. Lewis was a middle-aged strong intelligent black woman, and when she saw talent in black children she would force it out of them. She saw that I loved to write, so if there was a writing competition it was mandatory, I was in it, she saw that Yusef loved to draw, if there was a drawing competition he was in it, she pushed those with good enough grades to go to CVS high school for prep classes. It was like that for everyone in her class. She saw the MC in me before I saw it in myself.

During my 8th grade year at Caldwell Mrs. Lewis asked me what high school I wanted to attend, back then everyone wanted to go to either Kenwood Academy in Hyde Park or Hyde Park Academy near 67th and Stony. This is when she suggested Curie Metropolitan School of the arts program. So Curie it was, the school was located on the Westside on 49th and Archer. About an hour and a half bus trip on the Chicago Transit Authority.

I was iffy at first because I had to ride the 79th street bus by so many neighborhoods and high schools. Some of the schools were Simeon, Bogan, Farragut, King, Leo, etc. That's when niggas would jump on a brother, ten-to-one to take his Starter jacket or his Jordan's. There was another contributing factor on why I went to Curie across town.

In Chicago you had two major gangs the Folks and Moes AKA the Disciples and Vice Lords. The Disciples ran the Englewood area and the Vice Lords ran the southeast side. In the hood you always had those bad asses. Over by 87th street you had the *white house*, with Andre, Butch, Devolin, and little badass Bam. You hated to see Bam coming; this little nigga terrorized the neighborhood. He was a little dude but you knew if you hit his little ass you had to deal with his big brother Devolin who was worse.

They really didn't fuck with me and the crew, you see we were those rapping dudes, so they pretty much left us alone probably because they knew that we would give them an entertaining performance at the talent show. But if we had a fresh baseball cap, and if we fucked up and didn't see Butch a block away and he saw us he might take the caps, but no violence.

But there was this one time after school this kid kept fucking with me so I kicked him and broke his Walkman, he said it was Andre's from the white house and that Andre was gonna fuck me up for breaking his shit. Andre was the type of nigga that wore a trench coat in the summer time, he was purple black, and wore an oversized cap that covered his eyes, I never heard him speak and didn't want no parts of him, I avoided Andre for months, so fuck it, I was willing to travel to the Westside to attend Curie.

My time at Curie was bitter sweet. Curie was a mixed school, Blacks, Polish, Hispanics, and Latino. It was my first real time being around white people. Living on the Southside you could go all day without seeing a white person. One day my freshman year in biology lab a white chick touched my hair and said out loud in class that it felt like Velcro, I was mad and embarrassed and since that day I never communicated with a white student my four years at Curie.

That school was a mirror of Chicago, it was segregated, and everybody knew their place. On a positive note there were many talented people at Curie; singers, musicians, drama majors, and then there was me, this B-Boy. The most positive thing I got from Curie was learning how to read and write music, nevertheless, I felt out of place. I literally suppressed my talent.

I focused more on my social life and sports. I joined the football and wrestling team and pledge a high school social club called the *Crunch Bunch* who hung out with a group of girls that called themselves the *Home Girls*. We did everything the kids do in high schools, sex, party, fights, drinking, but nothing too heavy. The Crunch Bunch had been around for a while and many of the older guys graduated and went to Grambling for college. Let me backup and give a brief history of the Bunch, as told by Bernard Muhammad and Emmerson Buie Jr.

(Chicago, IL)

During the fall of 1980, Coach James 'Smokey' Lilly worked with the defensive side of the football team at Robert Lindblom High School on Chicago's Southside. One day during practice the defensive players that were under Smokey's tutelage were having a pretty good day against the starting offense, which resulted in Smokey, almost jokingly calling them the Crunch Bunch.

The seniors, namely Captain Tim 'TJ' Johnson, starting running back Dennis 'DJ' Johnson, and Angelo 'Gelo' Maynard added credibility to the group of underclassman as the Crunch Bunch was formed. A few years later the Bunch branched off and the first brother at Curie was initiated.

The Crunch Bunch taught me a great deal about discretion, unity, and brotherhood. Shit was crazy; we would have done anything for one another. Many of the older brothers in the Bunch graduated and moved to Louisiana to attend Grambling State University. This was around my junior year and the time when I started thinking seriously about college. My senior year of high school came around and mom and dad was tripping because I hadn't applied to any colleges, so with added pressure I applied to Grambling State University and a few universities in Texas because I had some family there.

At that time some brothers in the Bunch would call every week from Grambling telling me about the good time they were having. You remember the 70's film *Cooley High*? Grambling is where Richard "Cochise" Morris was going to go on a basketball scholarship before his untimely death. In addition, there were those Coca Cola commercials with the Tiger Marching Band, and of course there was the legendary football coach Eddie Robinson. To put it simple, Grambling was embedded in my subconscious.

Chapter 3

Lock yourself in a room doing five beats a day for three summers

I HAD TO HAVE HER; SHE WAS SO VERY SPECIAL, SHE BECAME MY MOTIVATION, MY INSPIRATION. It is not like I'm soft or anything but there just comes a point in your life when you see something that seems impossible for you to obtain and you just go get it. I've been rhyming since I was old enough to talk; I had years of lyrics under my belt. I always wanted to get into the music industry, like anyone fresh out of high school I had my doubts, but when I saw her; now I had a reason.

Me and the crew from grammar school, Adero, Anthony, Mike, and Darnel, used to freestyle while driving around the city, mainly from the south side to the north side on Lake Shore Drive. We used to stop and sit on the rocks free styling while the cool breeze of the lakefront and weed smoke slapped us in the face. Afterwards we would to go to Bubble's liquor store on 93rd and Stony Island or walked around Hyde Park. Many times we would just hang in front of *Harold's Chicken* attempting to get someone to buy us some beer.

My brother's friends had a rap group called the Masters of Conceptions (MOC's). They knew I could rap, so every now and again they let me hang out with them at their makeshift studio in one of the member's basement...this is where I got the name *Concepts*.

We would play old R&B instrumentals into a pair of headphones while rapping into a mic plugged into the input of a boom box with a dual cassette tape player. There was one thing in particular that stood out about Chicago rappers...everyone had their own style. Chicago was unlike New York and Cali, the Chi hadn't made it to the big stage; we were in our developmental stage. The west side had their own style and the south side had their own shit. ...Now me? I was the quintessential B-Boy, I was line for line, lyric for lyric, verse for verse; I was a dope MC.

Grambling State University is a historically black college in Louisiana. Grambling is few miles north of Highway 80 and little over a mile south of I-20. It is five miles west of Ruston, a city with a population of about 25,000. Monroe and Shreveport are the nearest *real* cities.

Grambling is a small southern town full of southern values. Things I never heard of, like if you don't lower the volume of your radio when driving pass a cemetery or if you don't say "Yes Sir" or "Yes Ma'am", these things were considered disrespectful, a total contrast from the Chi Town.

The university had an enrollment of about 8,000 students, but the town had no grocery store, no banks, and no hospital. However, it did have a few churches, three liquor stores, and a fried chicken joint. The weather was different from what I experienced in Chicago. Chicago is very cool in the winter and very hot in the summer. But Louisiana heat was different; I guess it was not so much the heat but more the humidity that made it intolerable. It would be crazy hot and humid in the day, but dry and cool at night.

I considered the campus big. One side was nothing but dorms for males and the other side was the female dorms. The female side had most of the academic buildings. The buildings weren't in poor shape but they could have used some exterior reconstruction. My dorm was Drew Hall, we called it the projects. If you ever visited a project building in Chicago you'll understand why we dubbed Drew Hall the projects. I think Drew Hall had at least seven floors but the elevators never worked, do not get on it, you will mess around and get stuck! In short Grambling was country and somewhat slow for me.

Grambling is where I saw her, Monye was her name. It was my first semester in college, I was in my dorm room checking her out in an interview on *BET*; she appeared to be so down to earth but yet so beautiful. Caramel complexion, her hair was braided, her braids were shoulder length; she had on a close fitting t-shirt and a pair of jeans. She was very intriguing with a Lisa Bonet vibe. Now it is a possibility that I was star struck, but that world appeared to be a whole lot better than the world I was living in. At that point I made up my mind, I was finish with college, it was time to do something that I wanted to do in the first place; I only went to college to please my parents.

I came up with a plan to work my way into the music industry. I needed some money and at the time I was fucking around with this redbone from Florida, her parents had a little dough, she did what she could to help me out, she served me well, she was fine, and *very* outgoing.

I was cool with this brother from Shreveport, he wanted me to help him sell some weed to my Chicago people on campus, reluctantly I did, and all proceeds went towards equipment. On top of that I used to hit up every dice game around, a little something I picked on the south side of the Chi.

Next I had to find a spot to build my lab. I found a spot about 10 country miles from Grambling, in Simsboro Louisiana, deep off in the woods. One of the professors at the university made a one-room apartment from what looked like used to be a nice size storage room. I dubbed my spot The *Cabin*. The location was perfect, the closest people lived about three miles away, plus there wasn't anyone around to steal my shit! The first thing I put in The Cabin was a small refrigerator and pictures of Monye, no T.V., no radio, no outside influences.

My father was an avid music listener; he had some old equipment so I asked him to send me some vinyl, a pair of speakers, and his old reel-to-reel player. Next I hustled up on a 122mkll Tascam, I had an old Scott receiver, I got a Roland SP-700, microphones, headphones, and a whole lot of marijuana.

Little by little life as I knew it was changing. I was staying up day and night creating beats, writing rhymes, and smoking weed. I felt myself changing I had no time for school, the homies, or a clinging woman. One month turned into two, two turned into three, before I knew it the semester was over and I had all F's, I could have avoided it if I had only dropped the classes, but the music had me like a crackhead, I was only focused on the music.

That was it for school, I did not want to go home and hear mom and dad trip on my grades... and I didn't want the homies shitting on my dream, so kept quiet, and stayed in Louisiana for the summer. Just like that nine months had passed, nine months of creating beats, rhymes, nothing else, just creating good music.

I remember hearing goofies on the yard talking about me being on drugs because the only time they saw me was at a dice game looking bugged out, with a wild fro, nappy beard, I use to think yeah, I'm on dope all right, dope beats! No one would've seen me at all, but I had to hustle and scrape for necessities. You know food, rent, and weed. It finally came to the point when I did all I could in the Cabin.

I needed to go a professional studio to sharpen my product. Plus, I was ready to blow that whole Grambling setup. So I packed up and drove 857 miles to Chi town. I always enjoyed long trips; those were opportunities for my imagination to run wild. When I was a child the family would drive from Chicago to Mississippi to go see Big Mamma, I remember the stories that Mom and Dad used to tell me of an intransigent south, how and why they decided to move to Chicago. While driving to Chicago so much was running through my mind, I had that nervous feeling in my chest knowing that I had the power to change my life. That I could control of my life, that thought alone got me excited.

When I got home I hooked up with this white dude who had a high tech studio on the north side, I met him through the MOC's, he gave me a hook up on studio on time. He said he'd charge me $25 an hour and that we could workout the fee for mixing and mastering. My only concern was him having my *masters* but at the time my options were limited and my music lacked the sound quality. I chose my best five, I needed at least a 10 hour block, at $25 per hour, $250. I got the money from Mom and Dad; I used the money they gave me for school shopping.

After I spent the money, I finally sat down with them and we discussed my plans. Surprisingly they were supportive, once I had their approval it was on. The titles of my songs were, "Shady daze," "What's a Brother to do?" "Are you ready?", "Nia Long," and "Rents due." It took the entire summer to complete the EP which was titled *Conceptions of a Confused Man*. The theme of the project was a young black male addressing and asking relevant questions about life, with one party banger. Now that the project was completed, I had to protect my *intellectual property* which was the most integral part of the plan. I got the copyrights for my lyrics and music from the library of congress for about $35.

Now a brother was confident in his shit so I printed up a few hundred CD's, for about $500. I needed more money, so I began selling weed. Around this time police began tapping into mobile phones, so I stop calling marijuana weed and started calling it *Food*. Selling Food was very convenient because most of my customers were at this hip-hop spot I hung out at on the north side.

Chapter 4

Please listen to my demo

I DIDN'T HAVE A TRADITIONAL NINE TO FIVE BUT GOING TO THE CLUB WAS A JOB. You learn a lot from hanging in the club type of environment; you learn how to speak, move, drink, do drugs, and approach the ladies. That is where you get your swag, your style, or what my homie calls *swagatude*.

Some of the most important advice I got was at the club. Check this out, one night I was having a drink with a club promoter, he was an old head. We were taking shots and shooting the shit about how you should promote yourself. Dude was very heavy on having a quality press kit. He spoke on how many CDs he'll receive and how he chooses which ones to listen to. He said that if he got a CD with handwriting on it he'll put it to the side, but the ones with a press kit and printed text on the CD, he would give it a chance solely on presentation.

He also spoke on stage presentation. He asked me how long I think an unknown artist performance should be. I said 30 minutes, he laughed and pointed out that it's hard for and establish artist to keep the audience attention especially in a club atmosphere where there so many distractions, he drank his last shot of Courvoisier, lit a Newport and said 10 minutes tops then get your ass off stage. Needless to say, I took that advice and ran with it.

After hanging at the club all night I would go home to get a few hours of sleep. Then I would go to WHPK community radio station in an attempt to get my music some spins on air. This was a tremendous task by itself. Every day the small studio would be packed with MCs with the same agenda. I had to do something different.

On the weekend there was the DJ by the name of EZ Eddie. He had a show on Saturdays; I preferred his format to the one during the week because his commentary was dope and his interviews were insightful. His show slot was from 3pm-7pm. This particular Saturday I wanted to catch him first so I got the station at 12PM. I sat there for three and half hours, he was thirty minutes late but I was determined. When I saw him he had a crate full of records in his hands and some more DJ equipment in his trunk.

I approached him and asked if he needed any help, introduced myself and walked into the studio with him. We talked and I gave him some new music that I was working on. I quickly learned EZ's pet Peeve; it was when cats come to the studio to get their shit played with curse words in the music without radio edits. This was some more good advice. I took a trip up north to the recording studio and got all my songs radio edited, brought them back to EZ and to his word he played them and we're still cool 'til this day.

Now that my music was in rotation, I had to start performing. This was the easy part, while in grammar school I would perform in talent shows so I understood the importance of practice. I'm old school, so for hours I would rehearse in front of the mirror, choosing which songs to perform in what order, keeping in mind the 10 minute limit that the club promoter spoke about. After hours of deliberation I finally came up with a formula. I would perform only parts of each song with beats, breaks, and instrumentals, with the philosophy that if I did this at every show my music would eventually catch on, plus EZ had my songs in constant rotation on the dial.

I literally was performing five nights a week, for free most of the time at opens mics, MC battles, festivals, you name it. If I got paid for a show it was no more than $300 or whatever I could get off the door, I didn't trip on the money, my thought on it was this, I was getting $300 for 10 minutes, more then I would make working anywhere else. I would perform for two people or two hundred, it was a tedious process, but in a city of a million MCs I had to get my name out there.

The next phase was getting the music to the records labels; this consisted of getting addresses from CD inserts, reading books on the music Industry, reading hip-hop magazines, contacting BET, MTV, etc. My point of reference was *Everything You'd Better Know about the Record Industry*, written by Kashif, I kept it in my book bag like it was the Bible; it had info on contracts, copyrights, royalties; the whole nine.

I shopped my CD to 40 record companies, which left me with more than enough CDs. I couldn't depend on hearing from the labels, so I sold the rest from the trunk of my car and promoted my CD when I rocked shows, especially at the colleges and universities. Finally I heard from about ten companies, I only remember a few, Jive, Interscope, and MCA. One label wanted me to come in under a developmental contract and one had the audacity to suggest that I change my style, I graciously declined.

Chapter 5

New York, New York, big city of dreams

MY SENIOR YEAR OF HIGH SCHOOL THE GRADUATING CLASS PLANNED A TRIP TO MEXICO. On a perfect 75-degree night in Cancun, I met a young lady by the name of Tyler Love. She was there on a vacation with her father, she sparked a conversation with me and asked me to join them for cocktails; her approach was cool so I accompanied them.

They appeared to be *well off* so they decided to meet in Cancun on some relax shit. She worked for Bruce Smith's Jam Rite Entertainment. Bruce Smith was the founder/CEO of Jam Rite Recordings a part of Universal Music Groups. Jam Rite was like the Motown of hip-hop. Her biggest project was the motion picture "Jam Rite's Documentary on the History of Hip-Hop," she was the creative marketing manager and her father was the owner of an information technology consulting firm. We vibed, had a few more drinks, she gave me her info and told me to hit her up if I ever visited New York.

The labels didn't work out and the time had come for me to take it to the next level. I had exhausted all my options and contacts, well not all of them, I had one more, Tyler Love, but to do it right I had to give her my music in person. I tried calling her for weeks before I got in touch with her. I told her that I was going to be in New York, she was like cool, when I get there hit her up and she'll show me the town. So there I was again, my man fronted me a pound of that green, I packed up and bought a one-way Greyhound Bus ticket to New York.

That trip was damn near 20 hours! And if you ever took the Greyhound anywhere you know that was some wild shit. A 300 pound man smelling like bologna and salami cold cuts was sitting behind me snoring while an infant across from me was crying and smelling like three-day-old Similac and throw-up. The restroom...forget about it!! Every stop I had to step behind the gas station to smoke a blunt. After 20 grueling hours I finally made it.

I am from a big city and I have seen NY on TV and the movies, I heard about the city that never sleeps, the Big Apple. But it is nothing until you experience it. When I first arrived at the bus station it was around two o'clock in the morning. I walked upstairs from the bus terminal and was near Eighth and Ninth Avenue, I could not believe how many people were out there and the lights; there were so many lights.

Within minutes of walking the strip to Time Square two guys ran their hustle game, "hey, hey I got that gold necklace," or "hey man you need that dollar cab?" I was in shock but it did not take long for me to gather my bearings. I walked around Time Square, grabbed something to eat, I waited as long as I could before calling Tyler. I called her around 8am, to my surprise she answered. She was very receptive, she gave me her address, and I took a cab to her spot.

Tyler was a very attractive girl, but my mind was on my business, not sex. Around noon Tyler took me to the Apollo Theater in Harlem, in one day about five shows are taped. She introduced me to some entertainers, a few comedians, and so on. Later on that evening we went out to dinner and had some drinks in So Ho. Tyler explained her job in detail, we joked and talked some more. We planned on going to the club but she had just made it back it town and I was fatigued from the bus trip, so we decided to go back to her spot. I told her that I was going to get a room, she was like, "ain't no need for that!" *(She probably knew I came to NY on a prayer).* She lived in a nice high rise on 59th street near Central Park, the doorman was a young Hispanic brother, he greeted both Tyler and I like royalty, something I wasn't use to.

The ambiance of her crib was on some cool shit, African Artifacts, an extensive book collection, a crazy CD collection, and some interesting movies dealing with conspiracies theories. She handed me some weed and requested that I roll an Optimo. She played some classic Minnie Riperton and Rotary Connection's "Magical World". Tyler went to her room took off her black business gear, and put on some jogging pants and a t-shirt. We blew some chronic, I guess she could feel that I was tense; she was like, "just relax." She burned some Nag Champa Super Hit incense, and grabbed two New Castles, you know on some real cool out shit.

After a few Minnie's cuts I was chill. To be honest that was the first time I took time to admire her beauty. Tyler had pretty, dark skin and short dark curly hair. She was about 5'6 120 pounds, a nice small frame. Her smile was

so soothing with perfect white teeth. Her voice
was gentle and when she looks at you with
those pretty, brown eyes it puts you at ease.
Her laugh was special also, and when you
talked to her, she appears to be into what you
are saying. I mean Minnie was putting your
guy in the mood, but that wasn't what I was
there for. She asked me what I was listening to
in my CD player, I told her just a little
something that I was working on and that she
didn't want to her hear it, she begged "saying
that you can tell a lot about a man by the music
he listens to." I teased her a little bit then I
gave it to her. She took my CD and put it in her
player.

"NIA LONG"

*"Who was that girl that stepped in my life? Who
was that girl that made me live so trif?*

*who was that girl that made me feel so sad? Who
was that girl that made me hurt so bad?*

her name is Nia and her loving is long,

nine seconds with Nia now a brotha's on bone,

she had the type of body one can't explain,

when Nia come around I can't maintain,

oh Miss Nia why you do it to a brother, you say you wanted me just me no other,

the way we met it was kinda strange,

I saw her once, twice, before she asked my name,

I told her Strickland and she cracked a smile, she said, "I think it'll be cool if we chilled for a while",

damn! She saw my ring and said, "Oh you're spoken for?"

"That's fucked up, cause you're what I've been hoping for",

like that I can't let it end,"

"so here's my pager number and we can still be friends",

right then I knew I shouldn't done that shit,

I regretted the moment that I did that shit."

Tyler abruptly stopped the CD saying with a sarcastic look on her face, "so you get ass like that huh?" I laughed; then a more serious sensual look came over her face. She was like, "so that's the reason you came to New York?" She then told me that we would talk business later and kissed me with her full thick lips, soft body; sweet smelling ass.

She pushed me down, I remember how natural Tyler's beauty was; Tyler's nails were medium length, none of that fake shit. Both of her hands pressed against my chest, she then pulled her jogging pants off, I put both hands under her shirt and began to rubbed the small of her back and breast ever so softly.

Tyler pulled my shirt off and began to kiss my chest as I simultaneously kissed her neck as I slowly slid her shirt off. I kissed her beautiful face as her warm firm breast pressed upon my chest. I can still feel her warm tongue as it softly massaged my neck. I began touching Tyler between her legs as I started to kiss her forehead, her ear, her cheek, her nose, neck, breast, shoulders, her back- my tongue glided across her entire body and stopped below her stomach. I lived there for about twenty nonstop minutes.

Tyler put her hand in my pants and began to give me a massage, I pulled my pants off slowly, but don't trip I wanted to rip them off in a hurry. When I was done body exploring, let's just say Tyler returned the favor. When she finish I laid her down and slowly opened her legs, Tyler resisted that position and laid me on my back, she was so tight-she slowly went up and slowly came down, again and again, while on top she moved her body in a circular motion as she gazed into my eyes as she slightly bit her bottom lip. Now remember it has been months since a brother smelled a woman, yeah, that's right, I gave her the best fifteen minutes of her life!

After we had sex, made love, or whatever politically correct term you want to use, we finished the blunt and talked some more. Tyler made it a point to let me know that she was not "that type of girl" and that she was attracted to me since the night we met in Cancun. You see to me all women are "that type of girl," when a woman first meet a man she decides in the first 30 seconds if she wants to fuck, from that moment on it is up to the man not to talk himself out of the pu#@y.

Following that nonsense she asked me, "so what's your gimmick?" my response was "I don't have a gimmick!" I explained to her that I touch on being a young black man in America. "I'm not a baller, so I can't talk about balling, I ain't no thug but I hustle, I went off to college but that wasn't for me, I smoke weed, but who don't smoke? And if they don't they don't know what their missing, my gear consists of a watch, a pair of earrings, mostly blue jeans or khaki's, Timberlands or Air Force Ones and a fitted, so there you have it Harveyl Strickland, that dope MC from Chicago, Who Am I? Concepts."

Chapter 6

Gimme a chance man, I know I can rock it

TYLER RUBBED ME ON THE CHEST AND SAID CONFIDENTLY, "YOU ARE WHAT THE HIP HOP INDUSTRY HAS BEEN LOOKING FOR." She then invited me to stay with her, but she had to go to L.A. for two days, Tyler told me to make myself comfortable, and when she got back we'll go by the studio to checkout two cats on the label, AKA Jam Rite.

There was this cat that called himself Siah, he had been around for a minute, he's been grinding to the top, the other dude was Dawg, now he was blowing up ugly, everything he dropped was hot; Tyler told me that the man himself, Bruce Smith stops by the studio frequently.

New York, New York, big city of dreams, I was there for two days alone, you know what I did, made beats, wrote lyrics, and smoked, both nights I checked out this hip hop spot *The Apartment*. This is where all the dope MCs hung out, it was the pinnacle of the underground hip-hop scene. I took the A train to the Meatpacking District near 8th Ave and 14th street. When I walked by the club there were mad MCs standing outside waiting to get in.

Now it was about 6pm, so I'm thinking the joint opened at 8pm or 9pm. I walked over and talked to one of the guys in line. He told me that the spot opens at 10pm, and that they were in line to get on the open mic list. The Apartment was where unknown cats could rap on stage with national acts; I mean everybody who's anybody on the underground hip hop scene would stop by there, Mos Def, Medina Green, RA the Ruggedman aka Stanley Kubrick, Medina Green... To get on stage your shit had to be on point. One thing I admired about the underground scene is the energy and ambition of an unsigned artist, on the real in one night you will fuck around and walk out of an underground spot with 50 flyers, 50 CDs, and 10 press kits in your hand.

When I stepped into the spot, it was like my first time having sex, I was in New York the Mecca of hip-hop. I sat there at the bar all night peeking niggas styles, stage presence, vocals, how they held the mic, rocked the mic, how they walked, talked, mingled. Shit, I was catching the feeling. Those two days Tyler was gone were filled with writing more rhymes in the daytime and lounging at club at night.

Tyler was cool as hell, but in my life I've met a lot of cool broads. When she got back from L.A., she showed me more of New York, introduced me to a few folks, and took me to one of the label's recording studio. Errol Seals AKA "Dawg" was recording his second CD in one year, the first time a rapper ever did that. "His debut joint went double platinum, predictions say his sophomore project would do just as well," Tyler said looking at me like this could be you.

Dawg emerged from the sound room, wearing a white Jam Rite t-shirt, black jogging pants, classic white Air Force Ones and a cold smile. This guy was on some Tupac shit, he was on everybody's joint; he was the hottest MC in New York. Some other cats were there, they called themselves *Rugged & Raw*; you know-the crew on deck.

Dawg was overlapping his vocals, his overlaps were different from what I've heard before, overlapping is when you rap/sing over, add, or double up your vocals. The greatest overlappers are Marvin Gaye, Michael Jackson, and most recently Lauran Hill. While the engineer was mixing down the overlaps, Tyler introduced me to Dawg, he rolled one, and we talked shit. We talked about Chicago, the hip-hop scene, and that he had met some good brothers from the Chi. We started talking styles, and flows,...Dawg was speaking his view on this music shit and how he used it, he was like, "I got so much sickness inside, it's like anything can trigger this shit at anytime, and my sickness is deadly...speaking of flows, Strickland right?"   "Yeah but call me Concepts,"   "Cool, Concepts it is, drop some lyrics after the session?"   I couldn't refuse the offer, I hit'em with "Chicago Renaissance."

"Chicago Renaissance"

Get that monkey off my back, who the fuck is that?

At my door this time of morning, like killa bees, I be

swarming,

Sit back relax, while I tax MC's like the government

hoes be loving it, I drop rhymes for the fuck of it,

MCs be watching me like a drama, fuck all whack

MCs, wannabes and they mamas,

no disrespect to the elderly, but the oldest MC can't

compare to me,

I need a rim shot, cause I rock the party 'till your

bottom drop,

I smoke bud by the dub, and drink Hennessy by the

shots, big ups to my true niggas, and to those phony

niggas no props,

and to those fake tricks, you can eat a fat dick,

Concepts styles be tasty like spaghetti and fish,

on a Friday night, I be blowing up like Value Jet

flights,

I keep your head bobbing like a hoe slobbing, on my

knob and,

I be mobbing with my crew, riches is what we

pursue, while I leave whack crews in a trance like I

knew voodoo, now what your gonna do?

Jump up and act like a fool on crack? Step the fuck

back!

Give me three peat, like "Da Bulls", I'll beat the

Heat,

in a seven game series whack M.C.'S cant' get near

me, let along hear me!

      I spent the next week going to the studio with Dawg, I set up shop in Tyler's crib, so when I wasn't at the studio, I was working at her spot, and if wasn't working at her spot I was at the club. Tyler would come home from work and just listen to me go in. Sometimes I would have something cooked when she got there, which wasn't a problem cause I enjoyed cooking, I would get the munchies, and not to mention I was lamping at her spot. Some days Tyler would bring something home or try to talk me into going out to eat, now that I think about it she never cooked, probably didn't know how or she was on some career/independent woman shit, which was cool too.

By now the word was getting around about this nice kid from Chicago who is fucking around with Dawg. I wanted to meet Bruce, but I wanted him to hear about me before we actually met, and I knew he knew that I was using his studio. I was allowed to use the studio after Dawg, this allowed me to study the engineer's, and Dawg's style. The second week at the studio Messiah, or Siah as we called him, came by to scream at Dawg, he came by a few times before, he gave me a nod, but didn't fuck with nobody but Errol. I was checking how those two cats interact, they were a pair of cool regular dudes, and both were down to earth and most of all on their business.

About a week after I first saw Siah we finally sat down and talked, he was nothing like the media portrayed him, he was very business savvy. The conversations I had with him took me to another level, the best advice he gave me was music industry rule #4080… "Record company people are shadyyyy!" Each day I started spending more and more time on the mic after Dawg's session. I was already dope on the mic, but my skills were immediately getting cooler. In one week we laid down "Daily Ritual", the following week we mastered it. Siah even worked on it with us. Nobody really knew what we were doing and that was the way we wanted it. We were about to add some overlaps and mix it down. I have a vivid account of that day that changed my life.

Dawg stood behind the sound booth nodding his head suggesting that I rock it again, with more energy.

"DAILY RITUAL"

"It's been my daily ritual, to keep my supply of

rhymes plentiful, audio, digital, I'm hitting you

with dysfunctional family blows,

fake niggas aint got no clue and they don't know,

they get the hook like on Apollo, or the gong on the

Gong Show,

now aint that something, they say I'm fronting,

cause I got the flows, that keep the hoes coming,

money talks, bullshit walks, now y'all bitches are a

hundred miles and running,

and who am I?, I'm one with my Lord, with a pen

as my shield, and a mic as my sword, can you

afford?

To feel the wraft of my madness, the style I display

y'all can't have this, your style is poverty stricken,

while mines live lavish, I be the best like Travis."

When I'm in the studio I drop my lyrics in the dark, with the lights off, and my eyes closed, when I finished I looked up and noticed Tyler standing next to Bruce Smith. I came from behind the sound booth and Tyler introduced us, we shook hands, his expression was emotionless, Bruce said, with a blank look on his face, "so you the man who's been using my studio time, but that's alright because you are going to put Chicago on the map." He told Tyler to bring me by his office. Now I was thinking how long I should keep Tyler around... I was getting to the point where I felt I didn't need her around, but I had to be honest with myself, I liked her, she was cool, she looked out, and she knew the ropes concerning the music industry, I kinda' felt obligated to take her on the ride.

Chapter 7

Going each and every place with the mic in their hand New York, NJ, NC, VA

THE NEXT DAY TYLER TOOK ME BY BRUCE'S OFFICE AS HE INSTRUCTED HER TO DO. The best way to describe the feeling that day is prepared, the opposite way I felt when I first walked onto Grambling's campus. I read two of Bruce's books and multiple books on the music industry and contracts. Tyler was dropping little dimes on me here and there about projects that he was working on; one of them was his Philanthropic Arts Foundation. Tyler didn't stay for the meeting. She had to work on a marketing project around town and she respected my privacy.

Bruce was sitting behind a cherry oak desk in a black leather chair wearing his traditional uniform, a blue NY fitted baseball cap with an all blue V-neck sweater with the *Gene*'s logo. Bruce, being the true businessman he is, did not beat around the bush, but before he began to speak I acknowledged him and let him know that I appreciated "the man himself" meeting with me and not an A&R. The first thing Bruce asked me was if I ever heard of the story about the smartest man in the world? I reluctantly answered no. He proceeded to tell the story.

"There once was a young fellow who wanted badly to wear the title "the smartest man in the world." But in order for that to take place he had to visit an older gentleman who held that title. After a long journey in the mountains the young man made it to the doorstep of the old man. He knocked on the door, and the old man answered, "Who is it?" The younger man answered, "I have a question for the smartest man in the world." The old man opened the door looking perplexed and ordered the young man to ask the question. The young man proceeded to say that he had a bird in his hand and asked the older man if the bird was dead or alive. The older man chuckled and said, "if I told you that the bird was dead you would open your hand and let the bird fly free, but if I told you that the bird was alive you would crush the bird, therefore the truth is in your hand."

Apparently speaking in parables was one of Bruce's things, this was something that he frequented over the years. After that Bruce presented a verbal offer, he mentioned that if or when we agree on the terms he would have the contract drawn up and suggested that I have my own attorney review it. Bruce then began to give his terms; the label would finance unlimited studio time, living quarters, all promotions and marketing, promotion tours, clothes, and fees for sample clearance. All would be paid back with the royalties from the first album sales. I would see a profit and receive a portion of the royalties after the terms were recouped. Basically, I would not receive no monies until the loans were recouped and the company regained it loses.

The offer appeared to be pretty standard, but why accept the standard contract, my music wasn't mediocre. I counter offered by requesting my own publishing, by doing this I would collect more publishing royalties also I would maintain creative control. I requested a Key Man Clause requesting Dawg and Siah as my co- producers for my CD, in technical terms if either one of them resigned, or left the company, I could terminate the deal. I wanted my crib to be my studio; I'm more creative in the comfort of my own home. Why get charged for studio time? I also informed him that I did not use samples, and no clothes, I would purchase them myself. I wanted to go in 50/50 on the marketing/promotions.

Finally I requested a signing bonus and not an advance because you have to pay an advance back. I would use a portion of the signing bonus towards my marketing and promotions instead of having Jam Rite foot the whole bill, again I would have to pay that back. Bruce laughed and said he loved my ambition, and said that he could give me everything and some, but not the 50% for marketing and promotions, and that I had to use samples. Bruce was very stern when he said, "plain and simple samples sell records, and whatever amount you could put towards marketing couldn't put a dent in this multibillion dollar industry." What we worked out was reasonable.

He also stated that Siah and Dawg would have to make their own decisions, Bruce didn't mind Siah and Dawg working with me because we would all be on the same label, and the clothes was all good. *Gene* was Bruce's clothing line that he was about to introduce and he needed a poster boy. We worked a separate deal for the clothing line. It took a while but we finally agreed that I would record three studio albums. It took about two weeks 'til the final contract was agreed on by both parties. Tyler suggested an entertainment attorney. We met with him, we reviewed the contract, and I was assured that it was legit.

The next year was spent in the studio and going on promotional tours. During that year I kept my personal website and I used *48Bars* for my publishing company. Bruce had me on a hectic schedule; if I wasn't recording I was rocking some club or making appearances in this city and that city. It is industry standard to build a following before your shit dropped, if I wasn't doing that, I had to be at an artist event. There is one last thing I added in the contract. I wanted Tyler as my manager offering her 15% of my net earnings. She deserved it and I guess this was my way of keeping her around for my own selfish reasons.

Chapter 8

Are you that somebody?

BRUCE LEASED ME A LOFT IN MANHATTAN AND TYLER AND I HAD KEYS TO EACH OTHER'S SPOT. Sometimes she'd be at my spot asleep when I got there, talking about she did not feel like being in her spot alone. I remember staring at Tyler while working on my material, but I would never go there, something wouldn't let me. Most of the time I would be too tired, other times my mind would be on some other shit, or maybe I knew sleeping with Tyler again would really fuck up something good. I've seen shit like that happen to people too many times. Plus it was about time for me to meet Monye, I was hitting the hot events in major cities and if shit went as planned, what would happen once Monye came into play, what about Tyler? You see that spelled instant drama!

My name was out there, I was making appearances where Monye would be present, and I figured that Tyler would be at those same events. Now if I started to fuck with Tyler how would I have played it when I stepped to Monye? I was sucked into a quagmire, I didn't want to lose Tyler, and I didn't want her to start any jealous shit when I started fucking around with somebody else. Women are notorious for that bullshit, getting all emotional; to be fair some bitch niggas get on that same shit too! So I respected our friendship, and she did the same. Tyler was always there, and I know always is a lot, but she was there.

Up until that point I had not performed for a major audience. I completed 50% of my CD when Tyler mentioned *Amsterjam*. Amsterjam was an American rock festival based upon the concept of the mashup fad. The best way I can describe a mashup is when artist match up another artists song to their song. The songs are created by blending two or more songs together by overlaying the vocal track of one song over the instrumental track of another. Amsterjam got the name from its main sponsor, Heineken. The festival also featured a second stage for lesser-known acts; this is where I came in.

The festival was held on Randall's Island, the small island sat in the middle of the East River between Manhattan and Queens. Jimi Hendrix played there at the New York

Pop Festival three years before I was born. Amsterjam scheduled Tom Petty and the Heartbreakers, Foo Fighters, LL Cool J, Busta Rhymes, Tego Calderón and Yerba Buena to perform, but they needed the "next" act to perform on the second stage. I told Tyler I was with it. To get to the island you had to take a shuttle bus provided by the MTA. Tyler and I met up in Harlem at the intersection of 125th Street, AKA Dr. Martin Luther King Jr. Blvd and Lenox Ave, also known as Malcolm X Boulevard. Tyler was tripping because we almost missed the bus, because I ran to the corner liquor store to grab a pint of Hennessey.

Despite that little bump in the road, the performance went extremely well, and I was very satisfied with the check I received for the performance. The crowd was so diverse and multi-cultural; it kinda had a Woodstock feel. There were eccentric modern day hippies sitting in trees, freely walking around smoking pot, drinking, and leisurely laying in the grass. Finally…the time had come for my music to be exposed to an entire different crowd, and they were so receptive, that performance was exactly what I needed. After the festival, Bruce put more money into my marketing and promotions budget.

Near the completion of my CD, Siah was having his release party in New York. I went so hard on my project I began to feel wore out, the first time in my life I felt burnt out, so I was gonna past on the party. Tyler called me and hit me with the real, well really some shit I already knew, so I was like fuck it, I'll go. Tyler was like, "how are you not gonna support Scott (Siah's government name)? Not only that Strickland, this is your time to shine, and if those reasons aren't good enough, I want to be with you tonight, so what's up? Get dress, I'm on my way." How could I resist that? I kept my attire simple, I wore a black Gene t-Shirt with dark blue denim jeans, an all black Chicago White Sox fitted baseball cap, and the Wheat Classic Heritage Timberlands. Tyler wore the dark denim skirt set, with a red skin tight Gene Tee and some exclusive all black Nike Air Force Ones High Supremes with a translucent midsole and red outsole. How fresh was that??? You see that's what I admired about Tyler, we would go to these events, the ladies would be all glammed out on some gold digger shit, but Tyler would keep it classy hip-hop.

When we got to the club the lines to get in were crazy. Tyler and I went in through the guest list line, but if you're not on a list it can be a hassle to get in. First you have to pay at least $20 for parking in addition to your entry fee, there are always at least three lines. One line is the regular line that is usually wrapped around the building…this is the ladies free before 11pm line. Full of mostly young black females barely dressed excited about their chance to pull an entertainer, or at least a dude with money, but this line is really the $20 line because the club will hold the door until after 11pm. Then you have the V.I.P. line for $60, this line is full of guys that more than likely still lived at home with their parents and badly wanted the limelight, and finally your baller line for $100, this is, and you know it, those that specialized in pharmaceutical sales or had a decent 9 to 5. Now this is what I don't understand, why people would pay to get inside the club, and then pay again to get into a section of the club AKA V.I.P.?

When Tyler and I got there we were escorted behind the velvet rope into the V.I.P. section. Tyler had tremendous people skills, she literally knew everybody that was *somebody*. She was giving her spill all night, "Can we get Siah on your show?", "Hey call me; let's make this happen", "What's up? Meet my guy Concepts," Tyler continued from the time we arrived to the time we left.

There was heavy hitters there looking made blunted, some were loud and drunk, you know the drill, popping bottles of Crystal, Rosie, $300 bottles of Grey Goose and

Hennessy in a $5000 V.I.P section paid for by the label or sponsoring company, the DJ's screaming out people names while braking Siah's single playing it 10 times in a row. Then you have people finagling their way to be close to the artists, VIP bouncers flashing there little flashlight signaling that they're having problems with a wannabe. Most of the artists were flossing, of course Dawg and Rugged & Raw was there, them ATL niggas, man I like the Dirty South, at the time the South was really coming up, the group Outkast from Atlanta was holding their own in the industry. You see that's what the ordinary person don't know or understand, the club scene isn't real, it's a show. A person that goes to work every day can't afford that club shit. When you see artist balling like that usually the label is paying for it and charging the artist for it on the back end, all that glitter ain't gold.

It the mist of all the bullshit Tyler pointed out that Monye's camp was there, we worked the room and finally spoke to Monye's manager and a few other artists on her label, Monye was on her way. An hour later I saw her, she was wearing an all black strapless dress with a split showing her caramel thighs, she was more beautiful in person. I was so nervous I damn near hurled. Surprisingly she was by herself, I couldn't believe that moment had arrived, this is what I've been working for since that day I first saw her on TV in the dorm room at Grambling.

I could not hear or see anything around me, my focus was on Monye, I only heard a voice in my head telling me to keep it cool. I headed over to Monye's V.I.P section when Siah walked over to me. He had a wireless mic and he instructed the D.J. to turn down the music to get everyone's attention. Siah reminded everyone of his release date, sent shouts out, then he gave me my props... "my shit is hot, y'all know Dawg shit is cracking, for those of you that ain't seen or heard of this man right here," Siah grabbed me with great excitement and enthusiasm and continued to say, "this is my brother Concepts, now drink and be merry, because you are amongst history."

Siah threw me for a loop, we dapped, and I expressed my sincere appreciation, all the while my eyes were stuck on Monye. I proceeded over to her section, hollered at the bouncer, slid pass the V.I.P ropes, and made my way to interfere with her personal space.

I sat beside her, leaned over and whispered as soft as I could in a club atmosphere into her ear,
"Could I be that somebody?"

"Excuse me!" she asked in a shocking manner.
"I'm Harveyl Strickland, but call me Strick, and you are?"
"Why do you want to know?"
"Why do I want to know, hmm? Let me think? Well there are many reasons, but I'll only give you two, first of all I'm captivated by your beauty, second of all I'm concerned because you're over here in a room full of people by yourself."

"Well I guess that a good enough answer, my name is Monye Tranquil." Monye shook my hand and cracked a smile; I ask her again why she was sitting there alone.

"Honestly I really don't want to be here."
"So where it is Monye wants to be?"
"Not here!" Monye looked at me with a confused expression and said, "Wait a minute who is Strickland, besides the person Siah was pubbing up?"

I explained to her that I've been in New York for a minute and that I was originally from Chicago and now as Siah told the crowd, I'm the newest artist on Jam Rite."

"Chicago, that sounds more like it, I knew you were not from the NY, I bet ya when your CD drops you're gonna change."

"I don't plan to, shit I don't want to either, did you come here with somebody?"
"I came with a few of my girls and my manager, and you Mr. Strickland?"

"I came with my big sister Tyler. Come on Monye lets blow this spot. I don't want to be here no more than you."

"Let me think, It all depends, I guess!" She said with a seductive smirk.

"Cool, Monye, your pretty little self wait right here while I talk to my people to let them know I'm 'bout to breakout."

"That's cool I'll let my manager know I'm leaving and who I'm leaving with, where do you plan on taking me so I can let my people know."

"I plan on taking you on the most sensuous quest of the 21st century, but on the real, where is it you want to go, are you hungry?"

"I love to eat."

"I'll take you to my spot, if that's cool, and I'll cook the queen a meal worthy of her greatness."

"Sounds like a plan to me."

I located Tyler and informed her that I was about to split.

"I see you Strickland; don't get your feelings hurt!"

"Tyler you're tripping."

"Whatever man just be careful and call at your convenience, okay boo?"
"You got it Tee."

When we got to my spot Monye appeared to be a little more relaxed.

"So are you straight Moe, if you don't mind me calling you that?"

"I'm cool, and I guess you can get away with calling me Moe, and by the way Strickland I don't usually get down like this! Your kind of handsome, and you appear to be cool..but just in case, I got a 380 fully loaded in my purse... and I would unload the clip on your ass if I had to, I just want you to know that", She said in a joking but serious way, whatever way she meant it, I wasn't trying to find out how serious she was. Monye went on to say, that she hated being around phony individuals. I felt her on that shit and asked her where she was from and she told me Detroit Michigan.

"So that sweet girl image ain't really you? Or did your label create that image for you?" "No baby it's all me, I just enjoy singing, my first love is acting, I've been performing since I was a shorty, my mother and father divorced when I was real young. My mom remarried and didn't fuck with me and pops, so I used to act to hide my pain, dad was real supportive...taking me to auditions, encouraging me to sing around the house, putting me in talent shows...so I love the art, but the business side of it is shady, so tell me your story."

"I was at Grambling, but college wasn't my ticket... rhyming is in my blood, I love this hip-hop shit...basically I packed up everything and came to New York. The girl you saw me talk to is Tyler, she's like my sister, she looks out for a brother, enough of that, you should enjoy the meal, I got skills when it comes to cooking." Monye commented on my spot, "You live here, this is a studio, I never heard of anyone living in a recording studio!" I told her that I only needed the necessities, bathroom a kitchen, and told her the rest was for my creations." I asked her did she smoke.

"It all depends on who I'm smoking with."

"Well hit this, it's only weed, but it's that fire, and after the weed set in we can engulf my skewered chicken with papaya chutney and pasta. And what would be your drink of choice, Alize, Hennessey, Remy Red, wine?"

"Water will do me fine, what's that playing?"

"Oh that's a track I'm working on I haven't wrote the lyrics to it."

"It sounds sad, like it's telling a story."

"That's because it is, I call it "Israel." I never fully read the Bible, my grandmother would read it to me when I was a little…she used to always talk about the children of Israel. My mother made me go to church 'til I was 13, but I didn't pay attention, I played around, messed with girls, and slept during the sermon, but the story of Israel, from what I know sounds like Black people in America. When I was creating the track I heard my Grandmother telling that story, I don't go to church now because, I witness the phony individuals, and so I feel you on that phony shit."

Monye said with a shameful look on her face, "I barely went, I sang briefly with the choir, I only went because my aunt made me go, dad didn't go, he believes in God, but he said, ain't no preacher going to get him to Heaven."

Enough of that Moe (trying my best not to hear her drama), where are you staying while you're in New York and where do you live?"

"At the Ritz-Carlton, I'm living in Atlanta now, speaking of Hotels, I hate them, are you really up for staying in hotel rooms for months at a time?"

"I never really gave it a thought, I guess I'm ready, it's not like I got somebody waiting on me, it's only me, no woman, no children; taste this."

"Ummm so you're a regular chef homeboy?"

"Oh you got jokes!" "Moe do me a favor pick out a movie, the DVD's are to your right."

She was sitting on the couch with her feet tucked under her, she swayed over there to get a movie, with her sexy feet and toes, as Tupac stated, "she see me jocking, put a little twist in her hips cause I'm watching."

"You know Strick I should be in the movies; I would have turned *Loves Jones* out."

"That would have been fresh Moe, considering that was the dopest love movie of our time, so Moe who was in the wrong Darius or Nia?" She quickly answered Darius.

"How do you figure? Wait Moe, let me first tell you why the movie was so hitting, first the movie was filmed in Chicago, big ups to that, the producer is from the Chi, now Darius steps to Nia, Darius and Nia hooks up, oh...I forgot she really steps to him first. Remember the part in the poetry club in the beginning?" "Darius falls for Nia but they're just "fucking" around cause she just got out of a bad relationship, she hits Darius with her ex-man drama, telling him that she's going to visit her Ex for a few weeks in New York. Dude don't even send her a plane ticket, but a two day train ticket! Now the train shit could have been used for romantic purposes like when Nia was standing in the rain at the end, or when Nia and her friend road in the old fashion yellow cab, or when Darius and Nia road the motorcycle in the rain on Lakeshore Drive, or when they were chilling at the Buckingham Fountain. Now Darius wasn't obligated to ask her to stay when she told him that she was going to NY, I remind you, they were just "fucking" around. So like any brother he moved on to the next girl, Nia comes back expecting everything to be all gravy, but she sees Darius with old girl.   Now Nia is tripping, then rolls with Darius's nemesis, but after that love conquers all, and on the real that's why the movie was dope, the food is ready lets' eat and watch!"

Half way through the movie I asked Moe if she was staying, she responded, "Are you kicking me out?" Hell no, I replied.

"I feel sticky; I need to take a shower."

"There's a robe and an extra toothbrush in the bathroom, I'll grab something for you to sleep in. Now I'm thinking to myself, wow, Monye Tranquil is in my shower, my shower!

"Strickland, Strickland, "she called softly, it sounded liked she was singing my name. "Come here and, could you wash my back?"

"And you know it."

"You can't do it with your cloths on!"

I took off my clothes and stepped in the shower, there she was not a blemish on her smooth, silky body. The water was hot as it collided with my skin; the water from the shower continuously trickled down from her forehead, down her face between the crevasses of her breast. I grabbed her waist as we kissed long, hard and passionately. I turned Monye around, granted her request, and began to wash her back, as I pressed against her I washed every inch of her body, arms, legs, thighs, feet, and she washed every inch of mine. When we stepped out of the shower, I picked her up as water dripped from our bodies. I sat her on the sink while kissing her, gently I opened her legs as she leaned back against the fogged mirror, the bathroom was filled with steam because of the hot water that continued to run. Monye grabbed my ass as she moaned and groaned from pure enjoyment, the more she moaned the more excited I became, Monye licked my ear and whispered, "You know what I want from you? I want you to call my name!" She said it again, "call my name, call my got damn name!" I replied in a panting voice Mon---Ye, MonnnYEEE", she grabbed my ass and would not let go as she was sucking my neck like a vampire. After our climax, I was speechless, so I just stared in her beautiful eyes.

Later that night I didn't sleep, I just studied her as she slept, watching her as if I was her guardian angel, she was still my inspiration. After sitting there thinking for a while I became motivated, I smoked one and created some beats. It's crazy... but for some reason pu@#y will motivate a nigga.

The next morning I cooked breakfast, Monye woke up in a gleeful mood, and she had to go because her flight was schedule to leave in a few hours.

"I know my people are wondering where the hell I am, I had a good time, I don't want to leave, but, you know, here's all my contact information, I know you're busy, but maybe you could come to the ATL and I'll show you a good time on my ground."

Trying my best to keep cool I replied, "You know I'm going to do my best, my CD release date is in a couple of months, after that I should have more free time, but even before that I should be able to get away for a day or two." As I drove her to the hotel I revealed to her about when I first saw her on TV back in college, she tripped because I fronted when we met, acting like I didn't know who she was. When we got to the hotel, I offered to walk her to her room, but she suggested that I go ahead because she was in a rush, I pulled up to the hotel, she kissed me, and ran to her room.

Chapter 9

There I was giggling about the games that I had played with many hearts

AS I DROVE OFF, I MEAN WITHIN SECONDS MY CELL STARTED VIBRATING CRAZY, TYLER'S NUMBER POPS UP ON MY CALLER ID, I ANSWERED, "HEY YOU?" "Strickland, you used to be homey now you act like you don't know me!"

"Tyler, you're tripping'!!"

"So is she cool?"

"She's very cool, we just chilled you know", Tyler calling me like she is one of the boys asking me if I got the puss.

"So Tyler how was the rest of the party?"

"Same old it was cool, I'll tell you about it, get up with me later."

"I'll be there."

"Cool and Strick don't forget to go by to see Bruce."

"I will Tyler; I'll see you in a minute."

I went straight over to Bruce's office and he gave me one of his motivating speeches,

"Strickland, you are now a part of Jam Rite, and you are going to play your part to make Jam Rite a household name, we're building a dynasty, when our family prospers, each individual prospers, next year's Grammy is ours, wait until they see Jam Rite!"

Bruce expressed some more concerns then I broke out.

I went to the crib and chilled out for a minute, I heard keys at my door, "who that?" "Who else got keys to your spot?"

"Hey Tyler I've been meaning to ask you have you spoken to your parents?"

"They're cool, dad is about to retire, and mom wants me to come back home."

"So what's wrong with Virginia?"

"Nothing I just don't want to live there …Oh did Bruce?"

"I know he wants us to stop by the *Viaduct* tonight."

"That's right Bruce wants you to drop some shit while we're there, we already set it up, Errol and Scott are going to be there, Bruce is pushing for y'all to do "High Performance."

Tyler was acting very excited, "So are we gonna roll together? She didn't give me a chance to answer, "Okay just be ready at nine?"

When preparing for the evening I got into the habit of visualizing before a performance. I knew I was going to make my mark, spread my love of hip-hop through my lyrics. I mean rock shows the way Run DMC used to, I knew that my music was going to remain classic like MC Ricky D and Doug E. Fresh's "La Di Da Di", and for my shit to remain timeless like Run DMC's "Dumb Girl". I kept thinking about old school hip hop artists, old school jams that moved me like an old negro spiritual, it's my time, I kept saying to myself, I'm 'bout to blow up like a Value Jet flight.

Tyler and I arrived on the set blunted as usual. As soon as we walked in I saw Siah and Dawg at their usual spot, over to the right of the bar in the V.I.P. area flossing. Siah was signaling to Tyler and I to come over. Them niggas was ready, looking like tonight is the night y'all. The truth of the matter was that the Viaduct was one of the spots like The *Apartment,* just a little more Hollywood. Once you blow up at one of these spots, you're plugged. The addition of myself to Jam Rite was like creating some Chicago Bulls, Lakers, or Celtics type of shit, a dynasty, I mean what other labels did wouldn't compare to our shit, the industry was about to be on lock! When Siah and Dawg walked on stage the crowd went wild, usually the rookie would get the first and the dopest MC gets the mic last, but niggas in the rap game might have been older than me, but I wasn't new to it, so I got the mic last.

"HIGH PERFORMANCE"

"Yo Siah, hit'em with that Jam Rite funk it's time

for these rhymes to make our pockets look like they

got the mumps,

while we be concentrating on getting this chedda

competition lose limbs cause we're hitting hard like

Metra and I bet ya,

Jam Rite's funk is the sound of the ages versatile

styles, literally got pages and pages,

Meningitis our flavor is contagious you can't fade

us,

now I always knew it was gone happen, but I didn't

know when,

working job to job just to meet ends power, money,

call them bitches twins,

I want'em to walk with me I want'em to talk to me

each and every day,

the industry anticipating my arrival like the Y2K,

lyrical matriarch in the world of Babylon I'm the

millennium phenomenon,

so here I comma clones duplicate my style like a CD

burner,

much props to future MC's, my future sons and my

daughters,

setting your mine free like the ex-inmate Porter/how

I feel? Sorta

lyrically I feel imperial spiritually I feel I can work

miracles cause I'm a serial, killa

On the M.I.C a legend in my rhymes a lyrical

G.O.D.

I threw down the mic onto the stage floor, when I was dropping my shit it was like nobody was there but me was on stage, the crowd was going wild, heads we're bobbing, bodies swaying, all you saw was bodies gestures moving as if they were giving their approval. I ran off the stage through the middle of the crowd, chicks were reaching at me, nigga's were slapping me on the back, I made my way to the back of the club, I walked over to the bar and Siah was on stage talking 'bout "give it up for my nigga Concepts." Tyler met me at the bar, she broke my mean mug and was like, "you da man, your definitely the man, now let's celebrate!" Siah was on ten all night, geeked up knowing how much money we were about to make. "Now that's what I'm talking about, it's time to make money, and switch bitches, make loot and flip it, then get more riches!" "That shit there, that shit right there, I like, I like very much!" grunted Dawg. So there we were at the table with Siah, Dawg, Tyler, Rugged & Raw, an all-star line up.

As I sat there sipping some Hennessey, I began to feel out of place, uncomfortable, the atmosphere started to weird me out. And it dawned on me that I wasn't an aspiring underground artist anymore, now I was one to be envied. Our performance was dope but this spot was little different. I saw haters and felt their stares; I saw the mean mugs coming from wannabes thugs. The combination of weed, adrenaline, and cognac, had me paranoid. Although I was excited I was never slipping and always watching my back. Just like the niggas, the ladies were staring to, observing, and analyzing the crew. I was hyped, but I was still cautious, at that moment I felt my life changing. I mingled for a taste then Tyler and I rolled out and went to her spot.

The car ride to her spot was silent until Tyler asked me how I felt about the night.

"What do you mean how do I feel, that shit was lovely, it was like everything went the way it was suppose to."

"You realize that you stole the show, the crowd wanted you, and wanted more, when it was all said and done, the ball is rolling now and it's about to roll nonstop, are you ready?"

I looked at her like she was crazy and asked her, "are you ready to ride with me?"

Tyler called me Harveyl the way she does when she wants my attention.

"Don't call me that, you know I don't like to be called that."

"Harveyl Strickland you've been my guy when you was just Strickland, hell yes I'll be there if you let me, this business is ugly, I mean you can't imagine, so prepare for it and brace yourself."

"I hear you Tee, put on Frankie Beverly & Maze CD, turn off the lights, and come here next to me and lay down, a perfect way to end a perfect night!"

The next day I woke up to a call from Bruce,

"Hey Strick, man I love the project, and the word on the street in that "Financial Backing", the colab with you Siah and Dawg, that's double maybe triple platinum, if you don't hear from me and you have questions, Tyler will know. I'm aware that next month is your birthday we are going to set some something up with that in mind, I'm thinking of releasing "High Performance" for the second release, how do that sound to you?"

I'm thinking what am I going to tell Bruce Smith???? "It sounds cool, hey Bruce, I really want to hit Chicago and ATL hard, I got to get that Chicago backing cause that's home."

"You know I understand where you're coming from, but Strick you gotta think national, global, check this out, I'll give Tyler your schedule. Look over it with her, if you feel anything should be switched do it around those dates, O.K. you got every way to reach me, take care brother."

At my crib, studio, whatever you want to call it, I was flexing the Sony 62 inch TV, I had the internet hooked up to it, with the minicomputer camera & microphone connected to the T.V. monitor. As a gift I ordered the same hookup for Monye. I got a call blasting from my speakers. I peeped out of the bathroom and there was Monye displayed across 62 inches of the monitor, "hey thanks for the gift."

"You're welcome, and I see your using it well,"

"My dad was in town so I had him to hook it up, I was about to call a tech but dad won't let his little girl grow up so I let him do things like that, he loves that type of shit."

"I hear that, well I'm glad you're enjoying it, check this out I got some good news, my CD is about to drop really soon and my shit is John Blaze! I'm real satisfied with it, how are things on your end?"

"I'm going in to addition for Rollie Gray's remake of *Sparkle*, word is a few well known actresses, are coming out. There three major parts in the movie, but I 'm going for the lead role, so wish me luck."

"You don't need luck; you're Monye Tranquil, the job is yours already, it's our time, oh by the way, what do you have on under that t-shirt?"

"I can show you better than you tell you!"

"Hold up before you do that, when are we going to hook up again?

"I get my schedule today; I'll e-mail my available dates."

"Moe I really want to show you Chicago, and I want to kick it with you in L.A. and when you have the time perhaps we could get down on your ground in Detroit?"

"We can do that, Strick can I lie to you?"

"You can do whatever you want to me."

"Well in that case let me lie, I don't miss you, I haven't even though about you once since the day I left your place."

"I miss you too Monye, call me when you get a chance and don't worry about getting the part, O.K.?" "Kay Strick, I'll call you."

After the singles dropped, they shot up the chart like a bullet. And this is when I got booked the for Boost mobile concert series.

Rockcorps put on star–studded concerts for children that performed four hours of community service in their neighborhood. The night before the first concert I sat in my apartment in Manhattan reflecting on how I got to that moment and for the first time I began to feel home sick. The first concert was held at Radio City Music Hall. Radio City seated around 5000, during the walk through they had hired some folks to sit in the very few empty seats, regardless of the few empty seats it was the largest venue I performed at thus far. MTV was launching MTV2 a place to see constant, commercial-free music videos, the concert aired to launch the cable network.

After the concert I had interviews with every major hip-hop magazine most notably the Source and Vibe. The demand was so high I did not make all the interviews. Of course I showed up for the magazines with the largest circulation, but for smaller magazines the label sent them photographs that were taken months earlier and gave them a spin on the interview. I didn't enjoy all of the interviews. It was fucked up because it was like the interviewers were looking for some drama, asking question like, "how do you feel about such and such?," "Concepts, will your stardom out shine other artists on Jam Rite's label?" "How do you feel about the "West Coast?" I mean all types of crazy shit. Most of the interviews took place before I released my first video, the reason the first video took so long to come out, is because I didn't feel the first concept of the video, you know the routine, expensive cars, half-dressed women, drinks, platinum chains, you know the deal.

Bruce gave one of his lines, "don't knock it, unless you got something better." Just what I wanted to hear, I suggested to Bruce what I needed, which was this nice video producer Chris Jackson, they called him Main Man, because if he directs your video it's gonna be right, your shit is going to sell, which makes him your main man. Bruce was like cool, Tyler reached out to him, Main and I discussed my ideas on "Financial Backing". The Video was to take place in Chicago, with multi shots of the Skyline, Lake Michigan, The Sears Tower, and so on.

I wanted to fly over the city with my name in neon lights of the buildings in downtown Chicago. First I woke up from my slumber rapping while putting on some classic Air Force One's, black Nike socks, some Khaki cargo shorts, and a black Jam Rite hoodie. I walk out of the crib and begin to run at the speed of light and take flight, as I'm flying over the city I see mere mortals battling over the mic while the entire city is in turmoil.

My final destination is on top of Sears Tower, the mortals surrounded the building looking up to heed my word. I eventually come down and I'm greeted by those that withstood the battle in the name of dopeness, which are the members of the Jam Rite camp! I said it and Main Man was like it's done. We ran it across Bruce and he gave it a go.

The Jam Rite camp was crazy nice, damn near every rap act had there own production company, but my shit was gonna be the nicest, Siah's label Prophets Productions was on their shit, a matter of fact he was pushing out acts of his own. When it came to Jam Rite, there wasn't a label that could touch us. After the video came out, MTV came knocking at our door. They wanted an exclusive interview, they wanted me to host their hip-hop show, my video was on heavy rotation, and my joint was on every urban and pop station in every major city, most of the stations parent company was Radio One who Bruce had a very good relationship with.

I conveyed to Bruce that my music would move units without payola. Payola is the illegal practice of payment or other perks by labels to radio stations to put a song in heavy rotation. Radio stations would report spins of a song to industry publications such as sound scan which meant more royalties points, also the number of times a song is played can heavily influence the popularity of a song. But at the end of the day it wasn't my money or my company, it was Bruce's, so what could I say or do?

I really didn't want to fuck with MTV like that but they could give me the exposure, not to mention Bruce was the boss and that's what he wanted. Now Tyler was working her ass off for me and the company, if there was an event in any city that I was close to while on my promotional tour, she made sure that I made an appearance. If the media was there, Concepts was there, if cameras were being flashed, I was in the picture. My CD went platinum in one week I didn't have a release party so we decided to celebrate the release of my CD, it going platinum, my birthday all at once.

What more fitting place to have it than Chicago? We held it at the House of Blues, Tyler brought out the family, the homies from Caldwell and the brothers from the Crunch Bunch, I was surprised with the artist that attended because some real heads came out. Rakim, KRS One, Eric Sermon, Da la soul, Central Division, Madam Zanobia, BlaxOut, just to name a few. What made the shit so cool is we all joined on stage for a freestyle session, I mean, I was on stage as a fan in a cipher dropping rhymes with cats that I used to blow to at moms crib. I loved that shit, the crowd loved it, I mean the whole set up was love!! This was the night I became cool with Blax and Zanobia. This is when I saw another side of hip- hop!!!

Chapter 10

What goes up must come down

TYLER INVITED THESE PERFORMERS BECAUSE I RESPECTED AND ADMIRED THEM, I WAS A FAN OF THEIR MUSIC, AND FOR THEM TO SHOW UP AND SUPPORT MY RELEASE PARTY IN MY HOMETOWN-THAT SHIT THERE HAD ME ON CLOUD NINE. I knew that Tyler really pushed to get the party off the ground and I could tell she really worked hard to make sure it went smooth. After the performance everyone was invited backstage to partake in the party spread fully loaded with my preferred drink after a performance, an ice cold liter of Fiji Water, a variety of alcohol, beef skewers, banana leaf wrapped rice, salsa, grilled fish, crawfish, sautéed green leaves, shrimp paste, sliced green mango, and eggplant caviar salad. It was so love having old and new friends celebrating my success.

When everything calmed down Tyler asked Blax and Zanobia to join us so we could show them the city and knowing Tyler possibly setup some future collaboration. We toured downtown then road to the south side, to my old spot on the Lakefront near 51st and

Lake Shore Drive. We smoked and kicked the willie bobos, really Blax and Zanobia was dropping knowledge. That night change me. There I was flossing like I was a star, I'm not knocking my label mates but Blax and Z was on some different shit, on some real shit. BlaxOut was his stage name, his real name was Amere Dawson, Zanobia name was Nikki Write, Amere was from Brooklyn and Zanobia was from Cali.

Blax passed me the blunt, held his head down, pulled out a cigarette, lit it, and began to speak; it was as if the lake rested for a moment to hear his words. "Hip-hop is always seen as an isolated phenomenon. It is not seen as having any historical relationship with other black forms of art, that's why it suffered some of the disrespect from certain critical circles. Hip-hop is only going to do what the people are doing, people are like, why is hip-hop fucked up? Cause the people minds are fucked up, you can't have sick people and healthy music." He paused, took a long drag on his cigarette and proceeded to say, "We are out here spitting positive shit and people act like we can't do any wrong, like we don't get blunted, smoke cigarettes, fuck with the ladies, or even make mistakes, but that ain't true! I just rather speak on a positive note, we got enough cats talking about getting pussy,

selling dope, and balling, hell there's a war
going on and we got to fight with everything
we got! What's up Zanobia?"

Zanobia shook her head agreeing with
Blax and added, "This music game is so simple
but yet very complex, four major record
companies got the industry on lock-they are
the music industry. Universal Music, BMG
Entertainment, Sony Music, and Warner EMI,
which means that if they want garbage to be
put out, it's going to get put out, it's not like
there are more MCs that talk about *non relevant
shit* then the conscience MC, it's just we aren't
given a chance. This is America, a country that
was built on the blood of black people and
Native Americans, created by those heathens
that migrated from Europe, it ain't about rap
it's about society. Strickland we support you
because you represent real hip-hop. We
respect those that respect the art, and speaking
for myself I know where your coming from,
honestly speaking the shit you spit is hot, it's
different from the rest of Jam Rite's camp, the
way your doing it is nice."

Then Tyler said something that fucked
me up because her statement made a lot of
sense. She reached out her hand and I handed

her the pint of Hennessy I was sipping on, she took a sip and made a *face* as it went down and said, "we all must understand the game before one could master it, one must learn the rules of the game. Most niggas don't know how to do shit but rap, which is cool, but what kills me is that they don't try to learn how to do anything else. You see this shit all the time in sports, an underdog team is playing an experience team, in the final seconds, the underdog team loses because of a rule violation and the experienced team capitalizes from it. This is the view that I take on the industry and racism. The bottom line is this, black, red, brown, all people have to take racism on and as humans and as entertainers we have to do our part. It is clear that white America has the upper hand, and like any person, people, group, in power white America does not want to relinquish that power. There are all sorts of signs, all people of color are called minorities in America, but whites are the minorities globally, and besides minority is a belittling word, words like that fucks with your mind set. People of color, we got to understand the game; we must maintain and fall short of traps, what traps? Glorifying drugs, guns, sex, violence, broken families, incarceration, and all things that adds to the cause and the demise of our people. By understanding the game we the can revise the game plan. Now me, I'm not a preacher, I'm a doer, I'm out here trying my best to learn the game so I can teach those that don't know and watch my back as well as theirs."

I sat there in a daze staring in the dark at flickering lights on the seamlessly never-ending lake. I felt exhausted from the performance and a *buzz* from the mixture of alcohol and marijuana, but somehow I had a moment of clarity- thinking where did that come from? I've been kicking it with Tyler for a minute but she never hit me with something like that, at that moment I began to view her in an entirely different way.

By now the sun was raising over the lake, and Zanobia was ready to go, I dropped all of them off at the hotel and told Blax and Zanobia that I'll get up with them back in New York, Tyler wanted me to come to her room but I needed some time alone. A substantial amount of time had passed since the day I left Chicago to go the New York; I needed to spend some quality time with my parents. I tried to relax but I could not stop thinking about *that* conversation; I instantly began to see everything around me in a new light. I didn't sleep at all that night as I tossed and turned- I did my best to hide my stress from mom and dad, they were in a *good place* so I didn't want to burden them with my problems.

Tyler met me at my parent's house the next morning; we ate breakfast and then flew back to New York. While on the plane the conversation we had at the lake was still on my mind, "Wake up Tyler!" Did you enjoy yourself?

"You know I did -them guys, Dawg and Siah, they can't trip about the artist I invited, they both had dates they couldn't break, and they have to understand that this is your program. It's all love, plus you know I got your back, I gave them invites first and to be perfectly honest I think this worked out better for us because you just exposed yourself to another crowd, you already got Jam Rite's core audience, anyway baby you showed love for your hometown, they would have did the same for theirs. I also gave Monye an invite, but her people apologized and said that her schedule was full."

Tyler *knew* me so well. The entire night I never mentioned anything about my label mates not supporting me; but I did feel a way. From a business standpoint I understood why Bruce had three of his artist scheduled for different events. Nevertheless I was disappointed. I also wondered if any jealousy was developing towards me from Dawg and Siah. Her word of encouragement was her attempt to put my restless mind at ease. Tyler was intelligent like that. She was killing two birds with one stone-she was consoling a friend and relieving tension in the workplace. Deep down I didn't want Monye there. One of my character flaws is not knowing how to react when I have people from *different* circles in my life interact together-it always turns out disastrous. I didn't want to be artificial with her-I was relieved when Tyler told me she with wasn't coming.

I appreciated Tyler efforts, so I agreed with her, "You're right Tyler, what did you do after I dropped you off?"

"I finished that Harold's Chicken I had from earlier in the day and went to sleep, and you?"

"I couldn't sleep; I kept thinking about what we talked about at the lake, but check it what's next?"

"Lex Alexander is having a birthday party, so we're going to hit ATL tomorrow. So do what you gotta do when you get back to New York. Bruce got me doing a ton of shit, so I'll see you at the airport, I'll get with you early with the time and flight information, you should be cool, now leave me alone so I can get back to sleep, hey Strickland?"

"What's up?"

"Anybody ever told you that you talk too much?"

"Whatever man!"

When we arrived to New York I took that brief time to relax and meditate, I took a minute to get my mind straight, because that shit that Blax, Zanobia, and Tyler dropped on me was heavy. I dragged around procrastinating on packing while pondering over my life. Thinking about before I got into the *game*, in Chicago when I was growing up. I also was thinking about Tyler, I noticed on the flight to Chicago she didn't say much, and it was clear that something was on her mind. I messed around and got the flight to ATL time wrong, so when we got to NY I only had time to pack. Since I was going to Atlanta, I thought about Monye, and my mood began to change, so I gave her a call. She couldn't make it to Alexander's party, so we planned on hooking up afterwards.

It's was a well-known fact that Lex Alexander was the *man* in Atlanta-his party was fitting of his reputation.

Tyler pulled me to the side at the party, "Strickland we need to talk," she said in a serious manner.

"What's up Tyler is there something wrong?"

"I don't want to talk here, let's go back to my room."

"I'm suppose to be meeting Monye"

"Talk to me now Strick, please!!!"

Alright Tyler give me a second to call Monye, if she doesn't trip, and I know she will, I'll ask her if we could hook up tomorrow."

As I walked into the restroom I was harassed by the hustling restroom attended and the sound of music and voices was blaring in the background, "Monye hey baby, I'm at the party, can we hook up tomorrow?"

"Hello, hello, Strickland I can't hear you!"

"I'm at the party, can we hook up tomorrow?"

You could hear the frustration in her voice when she asked why I couldn't come see her.

"I ran into one of my grade school friends, so we're gonna hang."

"Strick you know I leave tomorrow night for Chicago we're about to start filming, just come after you kick it?"

"Moe I'll try but I'm already fucked up and I can imagine how I'm gonna be later, and I don't feel like fucking with these Fulton county laws."

"I'll have someone to pick you up."

"Monye I'll call you first thing in the morning O.K.?"

"Whatever Strick, bye!"

"Come on Tee lets go."

I heard the disappointment in Monye's voice, and I knew why. I guess she felt that she was making all the effort to make it work between us, when we did see each other it was when she would come to New York, and when she came she would ball. She did it not to show off, but to make sure that I had a good time. One weekend Bruce let me slip away and Monye hooked up a trip to Jamaica for us. We were on some cool shit, this was the first time Monye got really high with me, we smoked the entire weekend and I also found out that weekend that Monye was into that "white girl" AKA cocaine, she said it helped her cope with the issues she had with her mother.

101

That was the first time but not the last I did coke, man we got super high. On a humid tropical night in Jamaica Monye and I laid on the white sands listening to the soft sounds of the ocean, we reserved an isolated spot for us near the villa we stayed in. We arranged for a grill to be put out on the beach, I marinated some shrimp, chicken, beef, scallops, onions, bell pepper, red peppers, sweet peppers, in lemon pepper marinate mix with Cheyenne peppers. As I think back, I still can smell the aroma of the meal, ganja, the sweet smell of Monye's perfume, and the fresh smell of the ocean. As Monye laid on my chest, I felt crazy relaxed, so at ease, and it wasn't all about Monye, It was about just being away from the norm, the quiet, the peace.

So I guess she felt disappointed because I was in her town, her stomping ground, and I hit her off with some shit like I'm kicking it with some nigga. But Tyler looked and sounded all nervous and so I'm thinking somebody died or some shit, I had to be there for her, no fuck that, I wanted to be there for her.

I'm giving off nervous energy during the ride to the hotel; repeatedly asking Tyler what was wrong.

"I'll tell you in the room, stop getting excited Strickland."

"So we're here what's up?" I murmured while going into my bag to get some weed.

"OK Tyler, this shit is getting old what's up? I'll roll you talk!!"

"Do you remember me talking about a guy name Jason?"

"The dude you use to date while you were at Hampton, your frat brother?"

"Yeah, he's in New York."

I sat back in my chair, completed rolling the weed, scratched my head, thought about what she said, and was like "yeah o.k. what about this guy?"

Tyler hit me with, "well he asked me to marry him", I guess she wanted me to save her from doing some dumb shit. I nonchalantly asked her what she planned on doing. (All the time I'm thinking *Love Jones*).

"I think I'm going to say yes, Strick I'm lonely, besides you and work I have nothing, and I have needs, you and I spend a lot of time together but now that your CD is out Bruce is going to having me doing twice as much. Time we have to spend together is going to become less and less."

I have to ask the question, "Tyler do love him?"

"I love him enough to give it a try."

"You know I will always be there for you no matter what you decide, you gotta do whatever makes you happy."

"So that's all you got to say?"

"Yep!"

"Now I'm not about to sit in this expensive room discussing another nigga. I got another question, do you ever think about that night when I first came to New York?"

"Strickland I probably think about it more than you!" Why do you ask?"
"I don't know just looking at you, I'm wondering why we never hooked up again, it wasn't like that night wasn't the bomb."

"Well I don't know either, I guess we were always making moves, and really with you Strick although you was good, sex is the last thing on my mind when we're together, I feel your energy, I enjoy hearing you talk, laugh, I wonder do you cry, and man your my guy!"

"Well tell me this, do you think anybody believe the big sister act?"

"I don't know Strickland and really don't care, you know I'm attracted to you, it's very obvious that you are attracted to me, so that's some bullshit we're pulling, but we can't fool ourselves."

"Well since you're about to do the fool and get married, and I respect the family, can we revisit that night, Please?"

"Maybe I'm thinking about getting married to the wrong man."

"Marriage wow, that's some deep shit Tyler, come here, let me hold you tonight, and make up for the neglect, tonight let me be your homie lover friend."

I woke up early to next morning with Tyler's chocolate, smooth, soft, naked body sprawled across mines, I looked over to the dresser, and my cell was blinking. I got up to check it and you know it-Monye was blowing me up. I stepped in to the bathroom and called her, I heard by the tone of her voice that I was about to get drama.

"Did you and your guy kick it?"

"Whispering I answered, "Yep, it was cool."

"So you met him at the party right?"

"Ain't that what...wait hold on," I looked out the bathroom and Tyler looked sounded asleep, "hello! ain't that what I told you, and what's up with the twenty questions?"

"You're lying Strickland, and you're on some bullshit!"

"What in the fuck are you talking about Monye?"

"Don't curse at me and why did you leave with Tyler?"

"I kicked it with her because she left with us, check it out, give me about an hour and I'll meet you at the IHOP in Buckhead!"

I sat down on the bed, leaned over and put my face next to Tyler's, she started smiling because she knew I knew she was pretending to be sleep, she said facetiously, "did you get in trouble?"

I played it off like whatever and changed the subject.

"I'm gonna fly back to NY later tonight, I'll call you when I get there, so I'm about to get dress and break out if that's cool with you?"

"Cool Strickland go handle you business, if I'm not at home you know how to reach me."

On my way to meet Monye, I really was not tripping on nothing she was talking about, but more of what Tyler hit me with. The way she was talking, she was telling me to make a move, but hell I wasn't ready for no shit like a commitment, not when I'm just starting my career, the shit had me tweaking, I kept asking myself was she for real? , nah she's bluffing!

When I arrived at IHOP Monye was there looking sexy but disgruntle, so I figured I couldn't let her get the first word in- before she could say anything I asked her with the *twisty* mouth, "I know you don't got people spying on me?, and I know you're not tripping on Tyler."

"No Strickland, Mr. Concepts, someone mentioned it in a casual conversation that you left with her. I was tired but lonely, so I decided to see what was up with the party. I'm not tripping on the sista, I'm tripping on you, you didn't have to lie, I never lied to you, why did you lie, did you sleep with her? Don't answer that, I'm shitty because you came to

Atlanta to do whatever you to had to do, as if you couldn't talk, do whatever the fuck in New York!"

"All we did was talk, she told me that she was thinking about marriage, I didn't know that's what she was gonna hit me with, I thought somebody died or some shit, you're right I handled it wrong, but I was being concerned about a friend, a friend, nothing else."

"All I'm saying Strick is that I see more between you and her; either you think I'm a fool, or the both of you are in denial. I'll be working in Chicago for the next couple of months on *Sparkle*; you need to think about who and what you want."

"Moe you know that's you!"

"We'll see", she said as she kissed me coldly and walked out of the restaurant.

Now I'm sitting there thinking, what in the fuck are Moe and Tyler on? I was tripping because this was not like me; this shit was unlike me to care. I finally decided to go straight over to Tyler's crib when I got to New York. When I got to her apartment Jason was there, so I played it off like I was over there to pick up something. Jason and I were a total contrast. He was ultra conservative, he had on some slacks, a dress shirt, and some hard bottoms dress shoes, he was very cordial, and overly excited to meet me. Still I walked away from there feeling shorter than that little dude *Webster*, and this is when I realized that Tyler might be really considering this marriage bullshit, I also realized that women are like men, didn't she just sleep with me last night? While all this shit was going down, Bruce had everything ready to roll.

The following months I was constantly out of town doing something. I started to get caught up in the life. In the past I usually kept my drinking under control, but I quickly became a heavy episodic drinker. I found myself getting wasted more and more, on top of the smoking, I was doing coke, popping and snoring ecstasy. As a result I woke up many times wondering what I did the night before, and who was next to me in the morning, other times I would wondered where the in hell I was.

When I visited a city it was my unwritten rule to visit the universities; I was intrigued by college students especially the white ones. I also frequented the strip clubs. I would pay some stripper's rent that night, money wasn't shit to me. Being on the road, I started to get an "I don't give a fuck attitude," on some Tupac shit, "I woke up screaming fuck the world!"

On the outside it appeared that I was living the American Dream; but my life was drastically spiraling out of control. While partying with the white college students I began to realize exactly where I came from-the *ghetto*. For the first time in my life I saw with my own eyes only what I had seen on TV and the movies. I was meeting young white males that were home for spring break from their Ivy League Schools, who grew up next to golf courses in million dollar mansions with manicured lawns and indentured servants. And who was I? Nothing more than a *Court Jester*, a person employed to provide general entertainment. That's when I had an epiphany, I felt like a fool, ignorant, ashamed-I was hurt.

In a futile effort to hide my pain I became less focused on my music. I was more focus on sex, drugs, and alcohol, what I called *Killer Nights*. I was paranoid; I always had a gun on me. I didn't have an entourage, because I didn't trust anybody, so I didn't owe anybody shit! My spirits were low, I was becoming more and more grimy, but the media loves dramas so my CD sales were increasing.

"Killer Nights"

"A Mere Reality"

"I've been around before Boys became Hot,

been around before records became Ruthless before

Boys became bad and had beef with Pac,

now watch your girl cause I'll having her shaking it

for daddy at the club showing me love as I rub,

that ass as she pass by, spread them legs, shake them

hips, rub my head, take this tip,

smooth skin, sexy grin, short, stacked, tall, thin,

firm breast on a body that's thin,

step directly into a ghetto paradise six pack stomach

with caramel thighs,

where every nigga gets his pick,

twenty for a table dance thirty she might suck your

dick,

so enticing they'll take all your loot, topless, G-

string with the high hill boots,

exotic dancers prancing for the cheddar tip her rub

her, get that pussy wetter."

Part II: Going Up

Chapter 11

I'm on my Home

TYLER AND I WERE NOT SPEAKING OR HANGING NEARLY AS MUCH, ONE OF THE REASONS WAS SHE WAS NOT TRAVELING WITH ME AS MUCH. WHEN TYLER AND I DID TALK SHE DID NOT MENTION JASON AND I DIDN'T ASK. Bruce suggested that we hire a road manager; it was beginning to be too much for Tyler. I called on Mike, one of the homies I grew up with. Mike was enrolled in DePaul University's School of Business program. It worked out to be a mature business move for all parties involved. A contract was drawn up and the label paid off his college loans and agreed to pay for the completion of school when he decided to return. I knew and trusted Mike, so this was a good fit for the both of us.

I was not keeping in touch with Monye like I used to, mainly due to her being busy with her movie, my fourth and consecutive single reached number one, I was scheduled to perform at the American Music Awards, in a few months. A few weeks before the awards I went back to Chicago, Mom was tripping about me not keeping in touch and seeing my people, so I went to spend the weekend with my family, plus Monye wanted to see me. When I got there my Mom saw the wear and tear that I've been putting on myself. Dad was like, "slow down son, you can't live your life in a day." Mom sat me down and talked to me, you know the mother type of thing that makes everything all right, all she really wanted was for me to be healthy and happy.

I was extremely close to my parents. I guess being the youngest made us closer. Both of them were from Mississippi, moms from Clarksdale and dad from Jackson. My mother is from the Belton clan; the family is known for being rebellious and out spoken during the slavery days. Moms always told me that Belton's displayed attitudes and qualities such as honesty, perseverance, and a strong sense in caring for family.

My parents fled Mississippi sometime in the 50's during the *Great Migration* to escape the racist south; they were married for over 40 years. They were blue-collar workers, dad was employed by the railroad, and mom worked in a factory.

As a child I remember my father as very responsible and being a great provider. I really didn't want for much and pretty much got what I wanted. He was a very classy man that enjoyed the finer things of life. Very well dressed, a very diligent worker, and finally but not least he enjoyed his music.

He would tell me tales of jazz musicians he would see perform in Chicago on 47th street. After coming off the railroad he would sit in his room; pull out his records a fifth of *White Label* and began to listen to Billie Holiday and John Coltrane; a pretty simple man who had very little formal education but had his PHD in life.

During my parents' time, there were not many opportunities for blacks, especially in Mississippi. When they came to Chicago and got jobs with benefits; that was a good thing and for their children to go to college was a great thing, but to me, to work for yourself is the greatest thing.

My mother is my heart, she loves people, especially black people, and she believes in community. Two of her favorite lines are, "don't be afraid of your own people" and "why fight against each other when you have the whole world to fight against." As a child I would get so happy while sitting at the kitchen table; watching my mother sneeze from the seasonings as she prepared meals for family gatherings. Mom is a strong lady, and when my world is crazy she makes everything make sense. She would always ask me how things were going in the music industry, I would keep my response real *PG*, but she always knew when something is wrong.

Mom bugged the hell out of me about Tyler, asking why I didn't bring her back with me, what's going between us? While my mother was talking, I blocked her out because something very disturbing caught my attention. On WGN television station, there was a report of a rape and murder in the Englewood neighborhood of a black girl, 11-year-old Ryan Harris, and if that wasn't fucked up enough, a seven year old black boy and a eight year old black boy were accused of the sick shit. The city of Chicago, so much drama, so much pain, while watching the news, I realized how far I had removed myself from that harsh reality, physically, mentally, and emotionally.

I sat in my childhood room, the same room that I use to rap the words of UTFO's "Roxanne Roxanne", KRS ONE's "My

Philosophy", and countless other rhymes from back in the day, that's when I realized what's been bothering me. I should have been doing more than collecting money, and boasting about how nice I was on the mic, granted I was one of the coldest; it was time for me to evolve and take it to another level. The industry had me all salty and I was meeting more and more shady people. That night in Chicago with Tyler, Blax, and Zanobia, the shit Tyler dropped on me about marriage, the drama from Monye, and that shit about the girl getting murdered, all of it had my head spinning, I had to get my life back in some type of order.

There was something I had to do while in Chicago, I had to talk to Moe; I don't believe in burning bridges, because I build them, so I had to have some type of closure. Moe and I hooked up downtown at the Water Tower. We small talked about the Chi, and how the acting thing had been going for her, then we went back to her spot, she was staying in a loft on Michigan Avenue.

"Listen Moe, I'm not a bull shitter, and I have no reason not be honest with you. I think we should take it easy, back in Atlanta you asked me to make a decision, I have made a decision and I'm gonna step back. Right now so much shit is running through my head, I need to get back to Strickland, or I'm gonna lose everything, including my sanity.

Monye took a sip from her glass of Riesling and said, "I respect your honesty, you and I know that things between us haven't been right, and you're not the first person to leave me. Unlike my mother, you had the courtesy to tell me before you left, and anyway who wants the real Monye Tranquil, people only want the image, but that's cool, because you're still my guy right?"

"You know that Moe."

She went on to say in an angry manner, "Besides, I hate when a person stays in a relationship and they know it's over...you know that you're only in it in name only, I'll tell a guy that I'm not happy, and he'll say O.K. and won't do nothing about it. Or I'll stop calling, and he'll call, we'll get up, not because I really want to, but because I was used to the routine, but the minute I meet someone new, someone that sparked that interest, I'm out of that relationship, leaving dude alone, now he's all salty, accusing me of fucking over him, but didn't I tell him? So Strick no hard feelings, I'm glad you were on the up and up with me, because I didn't mess over you, and I didn't want to get stepped on. And by the way tell

Tyler no hard feelings." She did her best to smile as she kissed me.

After I spoke to Moe, I rode the bus and train all day around the city, downtown to the south side, and visited the old places I used to stay and hangout, Englewood, South Shore, Hyde Park, 87th street. Englewood was and probably still is one of the worst neighborhoods in Chicago. There it was in the 90's and in some hoods in Chicago, you can still see the effects of the 1968 riots, building were still torn down, morale was low, dudes slanging on the block wearing hundred dollar gym shoes living in a ten dollar shack. The whole atmosphere was grimy; you could smell blood in the air.

What made the situation worst, a few blocks over from the Englewood community was Marquette Park, a place where the Klan used to march and solicit in the late 80's. There was not a change in the community or scenery, shit stayed the same.

I began to reflect on the murder of Robert Yummy Sandifer an adolescent that was out there banging, accused of shooting a little girl then he got blasted. I also began to think about Lenard Clark, a 13 little black boy that got beat by a group of white boys in

Bridgeport the neighborhood of Mayor Richard M. Daley.

While in Chicago I really took time to reflect where I came from, and reality hit me like a ton of bricks. Chicago is a great city, but there's a part that is cold, violent and full of shady days and sheisty nights. I pulled out a pen and pad from my book bag and began to write while on the 14th Jeffery Express:

"I'm living in Chicago, the city that works,

that's where you'll find a liquor store standing next

to a church,

we're living in a world where wrong becomes right,

these are shady dazes followed by shiesty nights,

let me illustrate a picture of gloom,

because we're living in a world that's damn near

doomed,

when the rains drops fall that's the tears of my God,

it makes me asks the question are we doing our job?

Maybe so, but maybe we're not,

"A Mere Reality"

somebody tell me when will this madness stop?

Fifteen stories, but they ain't skyscrapers,

you better use the stairs don't trust the elevators,

now picture that you're living in the projects,

you're living your life in constant threat,

I got my days of joy to my years of pain,

always puffing on that herb just trying to maintain,

I guess people don't understand me,

I can't cope so I keep smoking mo weed,

I got no where to run and no where to go,

my mind is full of fatal thoughts and I'm dying

slow,

and that's a got damn shame,

look at the ghetto situation but who can we blame,

little babies are dying our mothers are crying, my

lady is shady, our brothers are buying,

into that genocide bullshit,

look at us killing each other making the government

rich,

things are gonna change one today so I keep my

head above water and I pray,

what do we do in this shady situation?

Poor living conditions second class education,

we shall overcome but we never came,

things never change they changed the name."

Chapter 12

It's not a mystery it's history and here's how it go

I GOT OFF THE BUS AND WALKED FROM 93RD AND JEFFERY TO 87TH AND STONY ISLAND THEN TO CALDWELL- MY OLD ELEMENTARY SCHOOL. I sat on the steps of the school and thought about Tupac and Biggie; especially Pac, would Pac and I fuck with each other if he still was here? Was everyone really out to get him, or was he a skinny nigga with a big mouth? But the more I thought about it, the more I was like, fuck that Tupac was the coldest, niggas was just hating, but the reality was he made some *bad* decisions, that ultimately contributed to his death.

Pac's persona appeared real, when he dropped "Brenda Got a Baby", I really felt where he was coming from, that's what made Pac special, he had the ability to make you deeply feel what he was attempting to convey. Every since his first CD "2Pacalypse Now" dropped I followed his career. Pac was dropping knowledge all the time, but at first I didn't fully understand.

The more and more I thought about it, I just knew that there was more to their murders, Pac and Biggie; raps most prolific rap artists, they were more than two rappers, they were our voices, not just the voice of Black America, but the voice of oppressed people.

Many may not have agreed with their messages, some even say they fucked up hip-hop. People talk about hip-hop artist talking about sex, violence, and drugs, but it is going on in our community and environment, just like Blax and Zanobia was explaining to me. I made it up in my mind to change, I realized that in order to change I had to research history, to learn who I am. I had to research and learn about the history of the world, of America, and most become intimate with God.

The first thing I had to do was accept my ignorance. I started to think of black people I'd heard of in history, but never took time out to study them. Individuals such as Martin Luther King, Malcolm X, Bobby Seals, Huey P. Newton, Fred Hampton, and just like that, they all were shot down and or arrested, just like Pac and Biggie, I asked myself why? Was their message so powerful they had to be murdered? My mind would not rest, the Tupac shooting really bothered me, who was behind his murder? What is being done to find the culprit? Then a voice in my head was like fuck Pac, I'm in and so don't fuck it up, I'm making money, rocking shows, fucking hoes, got a blunt I'm opening it, give me some weed I'm rolling it, give me a lighter I'm smoking it! A more rational voice in my head was telling me that there was something more out there.

When I got back to New York, I called Blax; we met and talked a taste. I expressed what had been running through my head, just as I expected he understood where I was coming from. Blax was like, "I can preach 'til the cows come home, but you gotta find the answers yourself about yourself, so what I'll do for you is ask you some questions, then lead you to some references. Where did the human race originate? Where did your people come from? Are you and your people free? What is freedom? Are your people oppressed? What is oppression?"

Immediately after our conversation I began my research, I began to read the Holy Koran, the Bible, the "Autobiography of Malcolm X", "Seize the Time", by Bobby Seals co-founder of the Black Panther Party, "The Isis Papers", "Egyptian Religion". I began studying Greek philosophers, Socrates, Plato, Aristotle, Chinese philosopher Confucius,

Alexander the great. I studied modern philosophy, KRS-ONE, I read Assata Sukur, I read so much, that's when everything started to become more clear.

I began to change, my though process began to change, my dress, the way I presented myself, my love for my people and all people, and most of all the content of my lyrics. What about my name, should I change my name? Harveyl Strickland, where did my last name come from? Did Mack Belton choose that name once he was free? Was his master name Strick, get it Strick-land? I thought about my father, he made a name out of Strickland, so in honor of him, I kept the name.

The more I read I began to appreciate life itself, the struggle, and Tyler. So here's the question how long does a man or woman expect their mate to be there feeling unsure before they leave? I was alone a lot, but when Tyler and I did talk, we spoke about my newfound views, she was there, but again it appeared as if something was bothering her, and again, I knew it was that she was tired of being there without any assurance.

Isn't being with someone or having them there without commitment another way of saying, "I might find someone better out here, so when I do I'm out of my current relationship?" And who was I fooling Tyler and I did have an underlined relationship, I knew it and she knew it. You see Tyler and I were not together in the traditional sense, but our souls were connected, what was taking me so long to admit it? Would I be crazy enough to let Jason marry my soul mate? It was all on me, two halves makes a whole, and if I wanted to be complete, Tyler had to be there.

Chapter 13

I'm a get on this TV, Mama I'm a, I'm a put shit down

THE AMERICAN MUSIC AWARDS WAS COMING UP VERY SOON AND I WAS FEELING LIKE A NEW MAN, I WANTED TO SHARE MY NEW FOUND KNOWLEDGE TO THE WORLD. I sobered up and left the liquor and drugs alone, my mind was clear, my writing became clearer and insightful. EUPHORIA was the first piece I wrote:

My Utopia state has fallen, could it be my fate?

it has more holes and gaps than the Ryan Harris

case,

biblical structures and skyscrapers are falling as if it

was Armageddon,

while my heart and soul is bleeding, I'm a dead man

walking,

but I'm not dead yet man,

it is much easier to do the wrong thing, than it is to

do the right,

it is much easier to die young than to live a long

prosperous life,

to incorporate things you have experience,

wait one moment, did you hear that?

I never walk alone; I walk with four spirits, riding

me, guiding me,

to be a better person, because deep in my heart I

truly want to be!

But those Demons are constantly at me won't let

me be the person I know I can be,

and do I know who I'm? Am I who I want to be?

Am I what you want me to be?

Or am I what she wants me to be?

I'm not asking for no sympathy just some good

advice,

see those Devils want to sex, then I think twice!

Wait one moment did you hear that?

There go those Demons again, constantly at me,

won't let me, be the man I know I could be.

     While researching my story, not his-story, out of all the books that I read, the Autobiography of Malcolm X was the most influential. Before I read Brother Malcolm's book, I never gave the man a second thought. When I did hear about him in the media he was betrayed as a militant. I do remember seeing the poster with him dressed in a suit peeking through some curtains with a rifle in his hand with the phrase "By any means necessary" across the bottom of the poster. The phrase by any means necessary came from a French intellectual Jean Paul Sartre in his works Dirty Hands. After I read Malcolm's autobiography I realized that he was like other black men in America, he suffered from oppression.

The media and government have attempted to belittle Malcolm's existence and to assassinate his character. Malcolm was a man with sincere love for his people, and as soon as he turned his philosophies from civil rights to human rights, as soon as he stopped talking about only blacks in America uniting, but people of color around the world uniting he was murdered. Malcolm felt that if the United Nations where there to protect countries in crisis, they should be doing something about racism in America. The same thing goes for Martin Luther King, "I have a dream," so many of our leaders have been reduced to just one phrase.

Our leaders have done so much and they're much more complex than what the media portrays them to be. They are great people that fought for not only their rights, but also human rights. As soon as Martin stopped talking about civil rights and began to focus on human rights, Vietnam, the tearing down of the Berlin wall, he was brutally murdered, this has happened to our black leaders and any person that seems to speak out against America or tries to unite the people of the world, they are assassinated.

I researched the revisers and publishers of the King James Version of the Bible, the Holocaust, which was a great injustice to say the least toward Jewish people, for any destruction of a people in a moral and social crime. The Holocaust is a misdemeanor compared to the felony act that was committed against the Africans that travel the Middle Passage.

I felt ashamed as I read about the Middle Passage; ashamed that I never heard about the Atlantic slave trade, I didn't know about Africans that were kidnapped, transported across the Atlantic, sold or traded for raw materials, followed by a life of slavery.

As I read I thought to myself about how we are reminded annually about the Holocaust and the 6 to 12 million Jews that were murdered. Every couple of years we're reminded with some miniseries on T.V., or some blockbuster motion picture, but when I think about my 150 million ancestors that died, the way they died, the feeling that came over me was a sick, depressing, and a discomforting one.

I studied the Islamic way of life, Rastafarianism, Christianity, the civil rights movement, and the Black Panther Party. Fred Hampton was head of the BBP in Chicago and was murdered in his sleep. My mind was spinning; it was like I was blind before, I began to see just how much I was getting pimped by the industry, by America. Finally my eyes were open about America AKA Babylon- I had to choose, I could fight with my lyrics or continued to get pimped or protest with my lyrics like the legendary Bob Marley and Fela Kuti.

I was developing a better understanding why certain things occurred. I now understood why black families were broken up, why some of us live nigga rich, ghetto fabulous, why we cut off all our hair, get perms, why we dress the way we do, why we degrade ourselves and other brothers and sisters, how other races viewed people of color. I now understood the self hatred that has been instilled in us subliminally and right before our eyes, a self hatred that has been taught to us in our churches, in the schools system, and entertainment.

The truth had been concealed from us in all aspects of our life. It has been not only hidden from us in America but from other people around the world. The question is why? In an attempt to deprogram myself it felt strange, because there were so many aspects of my life where I had to redirect my thinking. It was hard for me to be natural, to be who God intended me to be, because society would not let me be the man I knew I could be!

It was one week before the American Music Awards, only one person knew what I was on and that was Tyler. I stayed out of the public eye-when I emerged my new appearance was shocking. I let my beard grow, I let my hair grow, my gear pretty much stayed to same, but I rocked Chicago shit, t-shirts that had Chicago on it, hats, V-neck sweaters, cargo khakis, you know.

I also stopped rocking conflict diamonds AKA blood diamonds, I realized that many of my brothers and sisters were losing their lives over shit that we were flossing with. I stopped eating pork, beef, and poultry, my diet consisted of mostly veggie dishes and raw vegetables. I was contemplating what I was going to do for the American Music Awards; I knew it had to be revolutionary and standout.

I choose the AMA over the Grammy because the AMA is more liberal by nature. The AMA was introduced by Dick Clark to compete with the more conservative Grammys. The major differences are the AMA are based on the sales and the people, the Grammys decisions are made by an academy; like my man Flavor Flav said, "Who gives a fuck about a goddamn Grammy?"

On the way to the 24th Annual American Music Awards at the Shrine Auditorium in Los Angeles my phone was ringing like crazy, getting messages from this person and that person, I only accepted calls from Mike and Bruce. Tyler and I rolled to the ceremony together, you should have seen her face when she got into the car and saw my shirt.

On the front the shirt read P.O.W. (prisoner of war) in silhouettes of Pac & Biggie, on the back it read COINTELPRO. I explained to Tyler what the statement meant- COINTELPRO is an acronym for Counter Intelligence Program which was part of the FBI during the Civil Rights movement and early 70's. The FBI systematically surveillance and preformed a series of attacks on Black groups and individuals.

How I see it, Tupac Sukur and Christopher Wallace were a potential threat to the America power structure, with their lyrics, they had the ability to stir up the grassroots people, hustlers, thugs, niggas you see on the block. Hip-hop is a billion dollar industry, these two cats had a voice, especially Pac, he had a nation of oppressed young black men with years of anger inside, all Pac had to do was redirect his pain and organize the people, say rebel, fuck the government, revolution now!

Now America got a crisis on her hand, and don't trip white folks buy over 80% of hip hop music, therefore young white America are influence. Another thing that puzzles me is that the killers were never founded for neither Pac nor Biggie. In Pac's case several people involved in the case are dead and one went to jail. I just can't see it, a murder on the strip of Vegas during a Tyson fight, unsolved, don't nobody know what happened? So I'm wearing this shirt to insinuate that the government knows what happened to those guys, and if it wasn't the government, what is being done to find the murders? After I finished explaining it to her, she nodded her head in approval, but warned me about the possible repercussions.

It was my time to perform at the awards; I didn't feel like entertaining, I've been entertaining bullshit all my life! I took off the denim jacket and my shirt was on display, I began to speak-"I'm sorry if I'm disappointing anyone for not performing and if the networks allow me I would like to use my three minutes to speak. First, and foremost, I would like to give praise to the Supreme Being that made every good in my life possible, and gave life to everything that lives and moves on earth. Give props to those that give props to me, I even give big ups to the critics and the nay Sayers.

Society has put before us so many obstacles, our vision is blurry, when we are hustling, cause hustling is all we do rather rich or poor; when we're hustling for food, shelter, and cloths, it is very difficult to focus on what is truly important, which is inner self. I will be searching to fill my life and the life of others with love, for life is love, rid my life of negativity. I'm on a quest, a spiritual quest, a quest to find answers, to who Concepts is... to understand the true history of my people, of all mankind, to find what part my people play in God's plan, and then let the world know my findings.

As I read the Bible, it is becoming clearer and clearer that the Bible is telling a story about the original man, or as modern day society puts it, the "Black Man", my perception of the Bible has been clouded by the teachings of the church, my body is a *holy temple*. For the record I do believe in a Supreme Being and Jesus, for the Supreme Being and Jesus are one. But I also believe in Malcolm, Tupac, Biggie, and a million more others that died in the struggle, but all people are one with God, I use Supreme Being because there are so many names for the almighty, and I'm trying my best not to offend anyone. The Supreme Being is love, as I research my history my clouds are gradually fading away. In short my days of performing without substances are gone, I'm committed to the struggle... each one teaches one, one love!"

The producers and sponsors were outraged, the audience, had a mixed response, some stood up and clapped, others remained in their seats in shock and awe, some had that "what in the fuck" look on their faces. When I finished my heart was pumping a hundred miles a minute, my palms were sweaty, throat was dry, but I felt that I have evolved, broke loose away from the shackles, I felt free. My cell began to ring, this time more than before the awards, I answered the call from Bruce, "Strickland what the hell was that?"
"Bruce don't trip, I should have told you, but I knew you wouldn't give it the O.K."
" Listen Strickland, you can't ever say what I'm going to say or do, that's not your place, I think I deserved more respect than that, if you I had spoke about this before hand, we could have work this out in a way that it could have benefited the both of us!"
"Shit Bruce I didn't know!"
"Well what's done is done, we'll talk later!"

Bruce called Tyler after I finished talking to him, I knew he was about to give her instructions how to put a spin on my speech. Tyler was backstage with me and Monye was calling from the in the audience. Within minutes reporters bombarded the back stage and began to hound me asking questions about my statement, it was so crazy the network wouldn't let me accept my award for CD of the year. I didn't bullshit with answering the questions, I hit the issues head on. What I said to the reporters is what added fuel to the fire.

"I had to do it, drugs, AIDS, second class citizenship and lack of education runs rampant in poor communities, especially black ones, while black entertainers and athletes live lavish and turn the cheek, can't fully blame them because they know when they try to help their income stop coming in, and before someone asked what I have done. I'll tell you I haven't done shit but contribute to the problem, but that's gonna change!"

Concepts one reporter shouted, "Could you explain your shirt, P.O.W. Tupac, Biggies, COINPROTEL?" Cameras were flashing everywhere, "Sure I can, what are the authorities doing to find the murders of hip-hops most prolific artists, Tupac Sukur and Christopher Wallace? I personally question the authorities, while wannabes comedians make jokes about our voices as if Hollywood loves him, I'm not happy or satisfied, these awards are a small token of appreciation from the billion dollar industry, this is what we get for poisoning our youths and wives, call me a modern day *Moses*. The one that gave me life put me on that stage tonight and put those words in my mouth as if I was *Aaron*. Let my people go America, let my people go in Africa, all over the world, my people free yourself, oppressed people free yourself!"

I immediately left after I spoke to the reporters, I didn't attend any after parties. Monye wanted to see me that night, I told her that I didn't want her getting involved; the media would try to fuck it up for her. Her movie was about to be released and the industry is so funny they'll dog the movie because of when we're seen together. Tyler left with me and we flew back to New York on the next available flight. The next day shit about the award was all over the newspaper, headline read, *Let my people go!*

Chapter 14

I'm going to my media assassin

I WAS CALLED EVERYTHING FROM
A MILITANT, RADICAL, REBEL,
REVOLUTIONARY, COMMUNIST,
TROUBLE MAKER, SAVIOR … MTV
requested an exclusive interview, after they
aired a special, "Who is Concepts? *Conceptions
of a Confused Man*, CD title becomes a reality!" I
refused to be interviewed by anyone, I didn't
feel that the media could help me, only try the
kill me, kill my words, rearranged them to
sound like something else.

Bruce and I sat down and had a long
talk; we were cool at the end of the meeting, as
I was walking out of his office I ran into Siah,
he wanted to talk about what went down.
"You know the network said it was going to
ban your ass, my ass, Dawg, and everyone
associated with Jam Rite, because of your, not
mine's, but your remarks about the Jews and
the Church. Everything you do affects
somebody now Strickland, you're not just
Concepts nigga, people are going to look at

everything you do. You got to think about it like a family, or gang, if you're my guy I'm not gonna fuck with somebody close to you because of the simple fact I'll be hurting you, I'm thinking of you like family as a friend!"

"I feel you Siah, but what done is done, and that's what I was a feeling, are you finish?" "We still cool Strick, your just wild, a wild nigga, one!"

Later that day Monye called to check to see how I was doing, the media was eating my ass up, she suggested that I give an exclusive interview and explain my side of the story, she said that she knew a great freelance writer, a cool down to earth sista. I read an article or two by Shawn Knots, and I felt what she was talking about. I sought counsel from Tyler she basically said she agreed with whatever I wanted to do and that it couldn't hurt the situation any, so I said why not? Monye gave me her number; I wanted to feel Shawn out before the interview-I immediately gave her a call,
"So where are you from?"

"I'm from Lithonia Georgia; I've been writing for a minute, I graduated from University of Arkansas Pine Bluff."

"Do you write for a newspaper or magazine?

"I use to do it all but freelancing allows me more freedom when I write. I have lost money freelancing but if you give me the opportunity, maybe I could stick'em up and make some money back."

"Shit you sound cool enough for me, so how do you want to do this?"

"Honestly I would love to do this face to face."

"Well Shawn if you're as down as you sound I'll pay for the trip to New York, and me and my people will show you a good time."

Shawn flew in the next day and Tyler and I picked Shawn up at the airport, at first sight Shawn was a beautiful eccentric black woman, she had the prettiest smooth skin, a big bold confident smile that lit up the entire room and big bright eyes that shined like stars. Her hair was locked and it was a little bit pass her shoulders and her scent reminded me of Frank & Myrrh.

She wore African bracelets and necklaces; she had a long skirt and a t-shirt with a couple with afros dancing on it. Shawn just had a positive vibe about herself, whatever doubts I might have had, to see her put me at ease. We decided to go back to my spot and I cooked for the three of us. Just like Tyler and I, Shawn was a Vegetarian. I hooked up an Ethiopian vegan friendly dish. While I was cooking, Tyler and Shawn were talking. As I listened to them I got a sense that Tyler was protecting me by checking out Shawn, at Tyler's approval we started the interview.

Shawn crossed her legs took a slip of her green tea and said, "Strickland please begin where you want."

"O.K. Shawn here we go, if you're not part of the solution you're part of the problem, if anyone loves hip hop it's me, it's in my blood, but hip hop has become what everything has become that has been touched by the racist power structure in America. Hip-hop is a voice for my people; hip-hop is a style, a way of life, a walk, a talk, a culture. Hip-hop reflects what's going on with its people. I see hip-hop as a movement and I don't want it to make the mistakes that the civil rights movement made.

After the civil rights movement black people in America became nothing more than consumers, the movement did not demand financial equality. Prior the civil rights movement Blacks had to support other black businesses, but after the movement black businesses slowly began to die.

In the 80's and 90's corporations figured this out and exploited the hell out of it. Clothing companies, food companies, movies, radio, you name it. True, a few blacks made a few dollars but at what cost. The Blacks that made money were used to exploit their own people, but hey, that's the American way.

With that said I was tired of rapping about the norm, living for material things, letting society dictate how I should live, I want my spirit, my soul to ride me and guide me to be the person I know in my heart I could be. My soul was unease with what I was doing prior to the award show. Socrates, the Greek philosopher, suggested that to have integrity your mind, body, and soul should integrate as one. Your body is not supposed to control your mind, when your mind and body are out of order, your soul is not at rest.

Black people in America souls are not at rest. Are we free? Before we can answer that question we must ask what freedom is. Do we love? Before we can answer that question we must define what love is. I'm not free in America, and my love for America is questionable, although the concept of freedom is painted as a beautiful picture for other countries to see, the reason we're not free is because our minds are not free, our minds are in shackles, all of ours.

We are too occupied with living the American dream. And I quote Adams from his 1931 book *The Epic of America*: "It is not a dream of motor cars and high wages merely, but a dream of social order in which each man and each woman shall be able to attain to the fullest stature of which they are innately capable, and be recognized by others for what they are, regardless of the fortuitous circumstances of birth or position."

Shit sounds good in theory, I question that dream, because we're living in a harsh reality, it's *a mere reality*, a façade, because the real reality is a distorted one. I want to be the way God intended me to be, because he is my God, my peoples God, we're the children of Israel, and in modern day society why are we allowing senseless murders of our children, sisters, and brothers to continue without standing up as a people, as a society.

If a member of Pearl Jam were brutally murdered on the strip of Vegas the culprit would have been found and prosecuted, why not question the police' isn't that my right as an American? Not really, especially not today when the media can convict a man before his trial. Why don't more entertainers and other prominent Blacks speak out? Character assassination is what happens anytime we stand up."

"So Strickland, why at the American Music Awards? "

"Was there a right time for me to do what I did? Listen I never did anything of that nature before, to be honest I never stood up for anybody or anything but myself, God chose me! But allow me to go back to the question of freedom, we're not free, we're not allowed to dress, walk, talk, or live like we're free, the definition of freedom has been limited and accepted. We in America have reduced and compromised our lives to what corporate Americans say it should be, but how and why? I'll tell you why....the other gods, money, power, and greed! The so-called American dream has become more difficult to obtain. See I now know that no matter how much money or power a person might acquire the power structure i.e. corporate America has 100 times more and when something is given to you it can be easily taken away.

The power structure has people divided in so many ways, creed, religion, politics, but instead of us focusing on our similarities, we all are humans, children of God, but let me tell you that the forces out there don't want you to know that, and I refuse to be a part of this deceitful and distrustful game."

I stood up walked into the kitchen and tasted the dish when Shawn asked, "what is the agenda for the people?"

"The answer is to become free, be who you want, live how you want while respecting your fellow man and obey the laws of the Supreme Being. Love thy land if it was human, love, respect yourself and others, because we're all connected, limit, and monitor how we get our information, hold corporations, politicians, federal, and local governments accountable.

Dinner is served, hey Tyler please put more juice in refrigerator when you drink the last one, pardon me Shawn I gotta run to the store, y'all need anything? I walked out the door and left my wallet, I was about to open the door when I heard Tyler talking about me, I started to just walk in but I decided to eavesdrop.

"So Tyler what is your relationship with Strickland?"

"Strickland is a special is a person to me and everybody that meets him, he's a real special person, this music industry is crazy, but

Strickland has always been sweet, the industry has not changed that, we're good friends."

Shawn responded by saying, "now Tyler that's some B.S."

"No girl we met each other a few years back, Stick came to New York and we've been cool every since."

"Tyler I understand," Shawn said with a smile, "it's just that I see how you look at him, how he talks to you, I see something there."

"There is something there, I care about him, I assure you that we are only friends, I'm engaged anyway."

"With Strickland I hope, because if it's not him, you're about to marry the wrong guy, take it from a sister follow your heart and if he doesn't see, you got to show him, you're in love with him aren't you?"

"It's all over my face huh?"

"All over it girl, what are you waiting on?"

"I love Strickland so much as a friend I don't want to jeopardize that with a relationship if it doesn't work."

"Tyler he treats you so sweet, talks to you sweet and delicately, I'm jealous and don't worry, this is just you and I talking off the record, that's my word, go get your man girl!" I heard enough so I finally decided to walk in, "what are you two talking about looking suspicious?"

Tyler stated boldly, "we're talking about your ass."

Well I hope it was good… enough of that, ladies please be seated so I can serve the queens."

Shawn tasted her food, gave compliments to the chef and then asked the proverbial question about Monye.

"Monye is a wonderful person and entertainer, I heard she did well in *Sparkle*, she's really about to blow."

"Come on Strickland you know what I mean?"

"No I don't Shawn."

"Are you two together?"

"We're friends, now if that all that you have to asked me, we can stop the interview right now. Everything else we discuss from here on, I would prefer that it be off the record,

I know you're gonna write what you want, but if the article is not one hundred there will be no more interviews, you heard?"

"Sure man, on the up and up....You and Tyler appear to be close," Shawn said as Tyler began to smile.

"We are, Tyler is my homie."

"I can't tell that you and her are not together," she said while shaking her head, like who in the hell are they fooling.

Tyler was in a good mood and wanted to go out, "So are ya ready to hit some spots?"

"I'm going to let the ladies roll tonight, I'm a chill, I think I'll be boring."

"Cool come on Shawn, it takes me forever to get dress, grab your bags from Strick's car and we'll get dress at my spot, see you Strick!"

"I'll check y'all, be careful, and watch out for the unexpected."

Chapter 15

We just might be O.K.

ON OCTOBER 26, 1997, THE 39TH ANNUAL GRAMMY AWARDS WERE TO BE HELD AT MADISON SQUARE GARDEN IN NEW YORK. I was nominated for eight awards and Shawn's article dropped the same time the nominations were announced. The article was dope, I mean she conveyed all my thoughts precisely; the article was straight forward and most of all positive. The article appeared in the small but controversial Ozone Magazine out of Florida. I owe a world of thanks to Monye and Shawn, big ups to Shawn for putting it down the way she did. Her article put me back on, my phone was ringing again, and the label was happy, everything was back to "normal", but I was changed forever, the ordeal strengthened my passion for my God and my people. I saw the world in a new light and I viewed Tyler in an entirely new way.

I figured that I was going to take home at least one award, I planned on just accepting the award and not to bask in my own glory.

But the night of the awards that all changed and I decided to spit some knowledge, I wanted my overall tone to be *Love*. The first award I won was Best New Artist; I spoke about my state of mind when I recorded *Conceptions of a Confused Man*.

"To be honest when I was recording, I was confused, but now my vision is not blurry, I now know the answer is something I had in me all the time, the answer is LOVE."

The next award I received was Song of the Year for "Are you ready?"

"This award is for Chicago, for the poverty stricken neighborhoods, for the MCs that practice their skills in slanted back Sevilles, for the underground, this is for the love of the art and finally being recognized."

I figured that I was only going to win those two, but I received an award for Best Rap Performance by a Duo or Group for "Financial Backing" with Siah and Dawg. That was a surprise, the crowd really showed love, that was for my musical family, that award wasn't mine that one was for Jam Rite and Bruce Smith. I also won Video of the Year for "Rent's due" that was for the workers and hustlers trying to get that loot, who barely have time for the family. I came up with the idea for the video of having images of families from around the world, to show that we're all struggling to pay those bills, to eat, to prove that struggling is a human thing.

"Israel" was up for Record of the Year and my chances of winning were 50/50. When they announced my name as the winner the crowd gave me a standing ovation.

"Tyler, would you please accept this award with me?"

Tyler walked on stage like Nubian queen, dressed in a grey shoulder-less beaded Versace gown, diamond earrings, accompanied by her radiant smile.

"Tonight is the perfect night, Tyler you have been there from the very start and I want you to be there 'til the very end. For I know that fame and fortune is temporary, for *what goes up must come down*. But love is everlasting and nothing matters if you're not by my side, I'm telling the world that I love you, I'm telling you that I love you, my love for you has made it possible for me to love others and most of all love myself. Please except my hand and be my better half and make me whole." A small tear trickled down her face, as her body shivered; she looked into my eyes and said yes.

The crowd stood up simultaneously while applauding as I held and kissed Tyler Love.

After the awards Tyler and I got married and moved to Chicago, we stayed active in the industry, just not in the same capacity. We began to organize by starting an intelligent conversation addressing issues that were affecting us as Americans. Taking a cue from other leaders such as Brother Malcolm and Martin we focused more on human rights instead of civil rights. We also understood that there were other entertainers and athletes that wanted to do more but were afraid and didn't want any financial repercussions. Therefore we created a site online where anyone around the world could donate to the cause. Our agenda was very transparent for everyone to see.

We created a committee with individuals and groups with like attainments. The committee had people from all walks of life, inventors, and dreamers from every profession, engineers, writers, scientist, educators that came up with new and improved curriculums, poets, doctors, etc. These individuals were progressive thinkers. I will take a line from the Committee's manifesto, "the committee was created to be an alternative to the government, to assist the government, not to challenge to government." We kept an open line of communication with local and federal agencies to remove any suspicion of conspiracies.

We named the organization the "Unity Committee." Tyler and I used everything we learned and experienced in the industry to start the Committee. I had nothing to lose, what could anyone do to me that I hadn't done to myself? Was I afraid of being murdered; was I afraid of being assassinated? No more afraid than when I used to ride that bus on the south side of Chicago. I can't describe the emotion I felt as fear, all I can say is that the feeling was familiar, something that has always been there, so I just accepted it. Unfortunately, that's part of the survival instinct one develops when growing up in a hostile environment.

Of course the Committee was met with some opposition from the "status quo" and the far right conservatives, but what could they say when the message in our music and movies began to change from negativity to a more positive global message of the human experience? I get it now. Bruce told me that the truth was in my hands, so many of us complain and blame others for our short comings, but seldom do we take accountability for our conditions, that's just what the Unity

Committee did, we 'fessed and took accountability. I felt whole, I was a part of something greater than myself, I was one man from the south side of Chicago making a difference.

When I first got to New York, Tyler and I kicked it tight as hell. Tyler was down to earth, and she appeared to be very much on my team. Now that I think about it, Tyler never told me anything wrong, she never fucked over me in any way, and she has always been there for me. Tyler was my friend, I had guys that I grew up with, and you know I will always be cool with them because of time, but I never had "that guy," and Tyler was that guy. She helped me achieve my goals, we got high, and we got on some cool shit, she was a rider, I can't tell how many times we just sat up all night vibing, listening to the likes of Bob Marley and Marvin Gaye.

I once read somewhere that *friendship is essential to the soul*, I'm glad I woke up and realized the value of Tyler's friendship. As I look back on the brief but life changing journey, I realized that I grew as an individual, as an artist, as a man. I learned the true meaning of the word love; I learned the true meaning of the word pain.

At one point everyone was telling me that I was the shit, I was the man, my music was hot. But it was not revolutionary, and that was cool with the label heads because they didn't want my people to hear the truth. I can say I was blessed to have the opportunity to be revolutionary, and just like other revolutionaries before me; I can't be stopped, because through my words another revolutionary will be born.

The same way Bob Marley taught me through music to love all things and to fight for my rights, I will teach another. Just like Marvin Gaye taught me to perform, but not only perform but to attempt to open the minds of those who listen. Or Tupac Sukur, who taught me to speak about the social ills of young black men and women in America. Last but not least I learned from my peers and countless other revolutionaries that I have read about and the ones I met in the industry.

Tyler Love, she taught me how to love; she gave me the power to believe in myself and is partly the reason I'm the man I am today. When I left Grambling I was a child with a dream, nothing was impossible for me to accomplish. I had young goals because I was a young man. I never would have thought a night Cancun would so profoundly change my life.

I learned more about my people and myself in that brief time of my life that will stick with me forever. I never knew a love like this before. I have had so called love but nothing could compare to the love that I have for Tyler. There are so many people in this world that have talent, I'm sure there were a hundreds of basketball players that were better than Michael Jordan or better entertainers than Michael Jackson, better golfers than Tiger Woods, but what was the difference? The difference was the support; Tyler was my support. And to think she was there right before my eyes right under my nose, and it took me so long to realize it.

I AM AN AMERICAN, CHICAGO BORN — CHICAGO, THAT UNCOMPROMISING CITY.

My name is Harveyl Strickland and this is my story, a story about the trials and tribulations of a B-Boy that found the love of himself, his people, and a woman by the way of an art form known as hip-hop.

Thank you for reading *A Mere Reality* by PRINTHOUSE BOOKS: Author; Rollie C. James, Jr. Please leave a review; we would love to know what you think.

PRINTHOUSE BOOKS

Read it, Enjoy it, Tell a Friend!

Atlanta, Ga.

www.Printhousebooks.com